Nothing in Mel Lawrence's life could have prepared her for living in the Australian Outback. She finds creating her new life and establishing a sheep station far from the elite society she was expected to live in extremely satisfying. She has a wife, a child, and a dream she never imagined she wanted, and they are all she needs. Will she be able to hold on to the happiness she's found after seeking it for so long?

A K'Anne Meinel novella

Novels in Paperback:

SHIPS *CompanionSHIP, FriendSHIP,*
RelationSHIP
Long Distance Romance
Children of Another Mother
Erotica
The Claim
Bikini's Are Dangerous
The Complete Series
Germanic
Malice Masterpieces 1
The First Five Books
Represented
Timed Romance
Malice Masterpieces 2
Books Six through Ten
The Journey Home
Out at the Inn
Shorts
Anthology Volume 1
Lawyered
Malice Masterpieces 3
Books Eleven through Fifteen
Blown Away

Blown Away
The Alternate Cover
Small Town Angel
Pirated Love
Doctored
Veil of Silence
Malice Masterpieces 4
Books Sixteen through Twenty
The Outsider
Pirated Heart
Recombinant Love
Survivors
Inn the Dog House
Flight
An Island Between Us

Vetted Series:
Vetted
Cavalcade (Prequel)
Pioneering (Prequel)
Vetted Further
Vetted Again

Novellas in Paperback:

Mysterious Malice (Book 1)
Meticulous Malice (Book 2)
Mistaken Malice (Book 3)
Malicious Malice (Book 4)
Masterful Malice (Book 5)
Matrimonial Malice (Book 6)
Mourning Malice (Book 7)
Murderous Malice (Book 8)
Mental Malice (Book 9)
Menacing Malice (Book 10)
Minor Malice (Book 11)
Morally Malice (Book 12)
Morose Malice (Book 13)
Melancholy Malice (Book 14)
Mad Malice (Book 15)
Macabre Malice (Book 16)
Marinating Malice (Book 17)
Macerating Malice (Book 18)

Minacious Malice (Book 19)
Meddlesome Malice (Book 20)
Meandering Malice (Book 21)
Vaquera Safica (Spanish)
Surfista Safica (Spanish)
ケーアンヌ・マイネル (Japanese)
Maniacal Malice (Book 22)
Sayyida
The Northwood Lodge
Monitoring Malice (Book 23)
Marked Malice (Book 24)
Shanghaied
Outback Born
Outback Bred
Outback Heritage
Outback Yearning
Outback Native

Pocket Paperbacks:

Mysterious Malice (Book 1)
Sapphic Surfer
Sapphic Cowgirl
Meticulous Malice (Book 2)
Mistaken Malice (Book 3)
Malicious Malice (Book 4)
Masterful Malice (Book 5)
Matrimonial Malice (Book 6)
Mourning Malice (Book 7)
Murderous Malice (Book 8)

Mental Malice (Book 9)
Menacing Malice (Book 10)
Minor Malice (Book 11)
Morally Malice (Book 12)
Morose Malice (Book 13)
Melancholy Malice (Book 14)
Mad Malice (Book 15)
Macabre Malice (Book 16)
Marinating Malice (Book 17)

In E-Book Format:
Short Stories

Fantasy
Wet & Wet Again
Family Night
Quickie ~ Against the Car
Quickie ~ Against the Wall
Quickie ~ Over the Couch
Mile High Club
Quickie ~ Under the Pier
Heel or Heal
Kiss
Family Night 2
Beach Dreams
Internet Dreamers
Snoggered

On the Parkway
Stable Affair
Kept
Stolen
Agitated
Love of my LIFE
Quickie in an Elevator,
GOING DOWN?
Into the Garden
The Book Case
The Other Women
Menage a WHAT?

E-Book Novellas

Children of Another Mother
Bikini's are Dangerous
Ghostly Love
Bikini's are Dangerous 2
Sapphic Surfer
The Rockhound
Bikini's are Dangerous 3
Bikini's are Dangerous 4
Bikini's are Dangerous 5
Mysterious Malice (Book 1)
Meticulous Malice (Book 2)
Mistaken Malice (Book 3)
Malicious Malice (Book 4)
Masterful Malice (Book 5)
Matrimonial Malice (Book 6)
Mourning Malice (Book 7)
Murderous Malice (Book 8)
Sapphic Cowgirl
Sapphic Cowboi
Mental Malice (Book 9)
Menacing Malice (Book 10)
Charming Thief
~Snake Island~
Charming Thief

~Diamonds are a Girls Best Friend~
Minor Malice (Book 11)
Morally Malice (Book 12)
Morose Malice (Book 13)
Melancholy Malice (Book 14)
Mad Malice (Book 15)
Macabre Malice (Book 16)
Marinating Malice (Book 17)
Macerating Malice (Book 18)
Minacious Malice (Book 19)
Sayyida
Meddlesome Malice (Book 20)
Meandering Malice (Book 21)
Maniacal Malice (Book 22)
The Northwood Lodge
Monitoring Malice (Book 23)
Marked Malice (Book 24)
Shanghaied
Outback Born
Outback Bred
Outback Heritage
Outback Yearning
Outback Native

E-Book Novels

SHIPS *CompanionSHIP, FriendSHIP,*
RelationSHIP
Erotica Volume 1
Long Distance Romance
Bikini's Are Dangerous
The Complete Series
Malice Masterpieces
The First Five Books
To Love a Shooting Star
Germanic
The Claim
Represented
Timed Romance
Blown Away
Blown Away *The Alternate Cover*
Malice Masterpieces 2
Books Six through Ten
The Journey Home
Out at the Inn
Anthology Volume 1
Lawyered

Malice Masterpieces 3
Books Eleven through Fifteen
Small Town Angel
Pirated Love
Doctored
Veil of Silence
Malice Masterpieces 4
Books Sixteen through Twenty
The Outsider
Pirated Heart
Recombinant Love
Survivors
Inn the Dog House
Flight
An Island Between Us

Vetted Series:
Vetted
Cavalcade (Prequel)
Pioneering (Prequel)
Vetted Further
Vetted Again

LARGE Print Novels

SHIPS CompanionSHIP, FriendSHIP,
RelationSHIP
Erotica Volume 1
Long Distance Romance
Children of Another Mother
Bikini's Are Dangerous
The Complete Series

Malice Masterpieces
The First Five Books
To Love a Shooting Star
The Claim
Represented
Timed Romance

Audiobooks

Doctored
Sapphic Surfer
The Rockhound
Cavalcade

Pioneering
To Love A Shooting Star
Mysterious Malice

Videos

Biography of Books
Ships
Sapphic Surfer
Ghostly Love
Long Distance Romance
Germanic
Sensual Sapphic
Sapphic Cowgirl
Couples
Lie Next To Me

Sapphic Cowboi
Timed Romance
Readings (SHIPS)
Doctored
Veil of Silence
She's Coming (The Outsider short)
It's Coming (The Outsider short)
The Outsider
Vetted

K'ANNE MEINEL

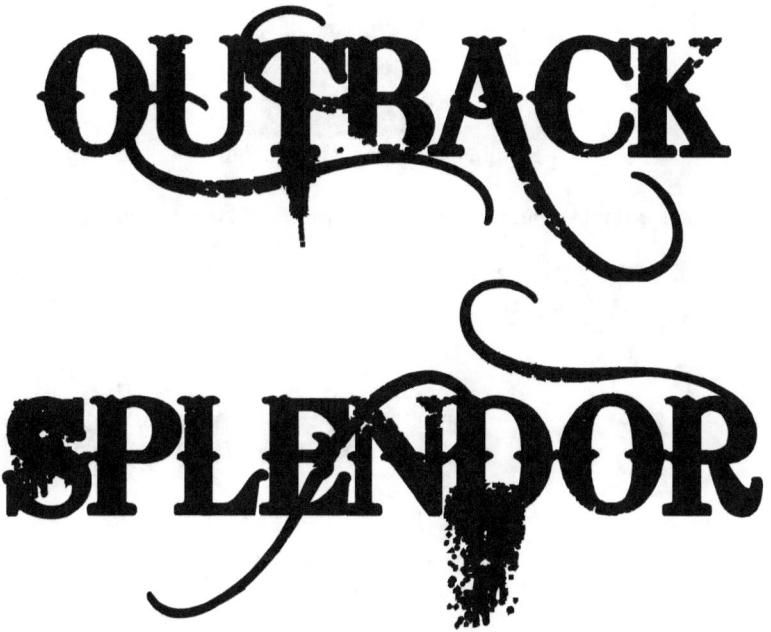

OUTBACK SPLENDOR

ISBN-13: 978-1733661195

K'Anne Meinel is available for comments at KAnneMeinel@aim.com as well as on Facebook @ http://www.facebook.com/K.Anne.Meinel.Fan.Page, Google + @ https://plus.google.com/u/2/+KAnneMeinel, LinkedIn @ https://www.linkedin.com/in/k-anne-meinel-a026385a, or her blog @ http://kannemeinel.wordpress.com/ or on Twitter @ https://twitter.com/KAnneMeinel, or on her website @ www.kannemeinel.com if you would like to follow her to find out about stories and book's releases.

www.shadoepublishing.com

ShadoePublishing@gmail.com

Shadoe Publishing, LLC is a United States of America company

Cover by: K'Anne Meinel @ Shadoe Publishing
Edited by: Deb Amia, Grammar Queen grammarqueen.com

Dedicated to anyone who
thinks I'm writing about them.
I am.

PUBLISHER'S NOTE

CHAPTER ONE

Mel looked at the long line of carts containing supplies that followed her and beyond that to the huge flock of sheep. Dogs flanked both sides of this valuable flock and men were posted at points. Next to her, her wife rode her own horse, no longer riding side saddle as she had learned to ride astride. Alinta found that gripping the horse's sides was easier than maintaining her balance on the side saddle she had previously ridden. In her arms was their small daughter, only a month or so old and thriving as she slept in the clever wrap that Alinta had rigged to hold the baby to her as she rode. This setup allowed the new mother to breastfeed when needed and kept the baby safe in her arms while also freeing her hands to hold the reins on the horse she rode. Mel was so proud of her little family. She saw the domed hills ahead and stopped at the top of one they chose to climb, taking a moment to

survey the rolling hills beyond these, where she had claimed her station. She saw the path the sheep had taken just a week ago, mowing the grasses as they were herded to Twin Station for shearing. Now, they were returning to Lawrence Station. Mel was proud that she had given the station her name and delighted that her wife and her daughter were returning to it at her side.

The long line slowed as men dismounted and began clearing the path using machetes, axes, and shovels. They were going to make a track into their station from Twin Station. It wasn't necessary across the grasses and around the spinifex, but it would be necessary through the brush and woods they traveled. Mel wanted them to make their way to the first of the permanent folds she had constructed to hold the sheep. She was going to leave one of her stockmen at this first fold with only two thousand sheep and a jackaroo, as they called the young, apprentice stockmen. She intended to split up her nearly eleven thousand sheep and separate them between the six folds she had built. She was also going to take advantage of the men who had come to work for her, some of them intending to return to Twin Station or head back to civilization when she paid them. She wanted a track to go from her various folds to the location where she had decided to build the home station. From there it would lead to the outside world and maybe to other tracks that would lead to other stations east of her own and eventually, Wilcannia. The men's wages and the months it would take to make this track would be well worth it in Mel's estimation. The track would make it easier to get mail and supplies, and it would eventually connect them to civilization. Mel wasn't certain that last

was a good thing but with a family to care for now, she felt she must open that connection.

The drovers she had sent for would eventually be bringing more sheep onto her station. One of the many letters she had written to her Sydney solicitor and accountant had asked that they obtain the animals for her. They would be able to get to the station through that far off track she intended to build. The builders that didn't return to town in the east when they finished building Senora Carmen Pearson's hacienda at Twin Station would be coming to build a home for Mel and her family. They would also erect barns, sheds, and other things she needed. She and her men would have cleared the areas she had planned for these buildings and stacked wood in preparation for them. In addition, they would start to fence off the corrals she needed for the large operation she intended to have. Having seen many operations and their setups on the drive to the Outback as well as observing the operation of Twin Station, Mel had very definite ideas of what she wanted for her own.

After discussing her needs with the builder and learning what supplies she would need from Sydney, Mel had written several letters placing orders and instructing her solicitor and accountant to pay for the goods and arrange for them to be shipped to her. Things were going to be very busy for a long time, and she was loving it. She couldn't remember another time in her life when she had been this happy.

Alinta could sense Mel's happiness. She was happy too, but she was concerned. She had thought the kissing she and Mel had done would lead to more. She didn't know what that entailed, but she

yearned for more than they had. She knew it might be difficult with all the men around and their constant traveling, but she wanted the physical closeness that she knew existed between mates. Mel hadn't said anything about it since their kissing, but there had been so much to do as they got the carts organized and the men and sheep headed back to the wildness of their own lands. She liked the sound of that…their own lands. Mel had named it Lawrence Station, and she liked that too. The men were addressing her as Mrs. Lawrence, and Mel had explained it was a sign of respect since they were now married. Alinta had never had a second name before, and other than her tribal affiliation, she hadn't thought much about it. She glanced down at her daughter. Ainia had three names now. She was Ainia Mary Lawrence. It was a fine name, and it was a white name, but Alinta wanted that for her daughter. Even she could see that her daughter looked white, and this made her mother proud.

They managed to cut through the brush to that first fold in a matter of days. Mel quickly started a fire, and Alinta got busy preparing a dinner for them all. Mel noticed and stopped her. She explained that Alinta was to only make food for their family and any honored guests. A second fire was started for the men. It was separate and well away from the hut that was still standing, which Mel had taken for her wife and daughter, wanting to get them out of the elements. Some of the stockmen had wives with them as well, and Mel had promised to build houses for any married stockmen who came to work for her regardless if they worked at the home paddock or out in one of the many paddocks she was building. That incentive had brought a few more stockmen out to work for her, but only two had brought their wives on this trip. A

couple other men said they would see how the position suited them before sending for their own wives and families. Meanwhile, they had their own supplies and stayed separate from the station owner.

Mel needed time alone as she thought about everything she had to do. She'd always enjoyed a challenge, so it didn't overwhelm her but seeing things coming together was getting her excited.

The flock was inside the enormous fold and camped out on the plain before it. The flock had grown beyond all her expectations and was too big for the single fold. She hoped next year's crop of lambs was just as large. Originally, the fold had held all four thousand sheep, but now, with their offspring beside them, they overflowed it. Dingoes had trailed the large flock, and the men had shot those they saw. Mel had given instructions to shoot all dingoes on sight.

Mel fed the dogs, praising them, petting them, and giving a little extra to the two bitches with pups. The pups had ridden in bags behind her wife's saddle, and the bitches originally followed the horse anxiously, but now, they were used to the setup and knew Mel would lower the pups whenever they stopped. The pups had nursed avidly and seemed to be thriving. Only a couple had died when the second bitch had given birth and a large pup blocked the birth canal. Since then, Mel was pleased to see those that remained growing rapidly. She hoped all of them showed an interest in the sheep because she'd have to destroy any that didn't. They had no use on a station for animals that didn't do the duties they were intended for. She wouldn't enjoy it though; she wouldn't bash in their heads as some grazers or farmers did. She'd probably tie them in the very bag she was transporting them in. After sewing up the holes and filling the bags with rocks, she would simply drop them in a billabong, what they called a pond here in Australia. She hoped it wouldn't come to that. Her heart wasn't in the idea of destroying any of the pups.

Her mind went over the path they would take to the next fold, thinking of the best and easiest ways around the hills and valleys and the route that would have water for any who traveled it. By then, Alinta had their dinner ready and hot from the fire. Dinner was rice and peas, mutton, and as a bonus, some type of fruit that Alinta had scavenged. Mel loved that her wife no longer ate grubs or grasshoppers. Just the thought of that had been repugnant to the white woman.

Alinta had noticed the faces Mel made when she ate things that were natural to her. Wanting her white daughter raised in the white man's ways, she had begun to imitate Mel, and this included her eating habits.

That night, they snuggled together and kissed, but Mel wouldn't let it go any further. The men and women who traveled with her were only feet away at the other fire, and she wanted no sounds carrying on the night air. She also wondered if Alinta might still be sore from having given birth to their daughter. She knew a lot of women were in bed for weeks, if not months, before and after the birth. Still, this healthy woman didn't even look like she had ever been pregnant. Sometime during the night, Mel woke when Ainia started fussing. Alinta rose to change the baby, shushing her with crooning sounds and then feeding her. Mel saw the silhouette of her wife outlined against the backdrop of the bright moon. She could feel the lust building within her. She wanted to touch her wife, especially when she came

back to bed, but instead, she resisted and finally was able to fall back to sleep.

Everyone was up before dawn. Some of the men began to clear brush from the path that would become the trail that wound between the folds, getting a head start before the others. Some began to harness the bullocks they were using with the carts that carried all the supplies Mel had ordered. Mel portioned out some supplies for the stockman that was remaining behind, leaving enough to last several weeks for the man and his jackaroo. She wondered if wagons instead of carts would someday be used on these tracks. She couldn't imagine that there would ever be roads out here in the Outback.

CHAPTER TWO

It took them weeks to cut the tracks to the home station. By then, there were no more sheep to attend to as they had left the last of them in the fold nearest the homesite. The men began girding and felling trees, building up a supply for the house, barns, and sheds they would need.

"Does anyone know how to measure off for the buildings?" Mel asked, and two men volunteered to show her.

They unrolled string to the desired lengths. Mel was planning large buildings for their future uses, marking off where everything would go with stakes.

They began the building with the bunkhouse for all the unmarried stockmen. They called them barracks down here, and she tried to remember that. She wanted the barracks large enough to house at least two dozen men or more. They rolled rocks and boulders into place for the base, not needing stilts to keep out water and bugs. Another one of the men discovered clay in her hidden valley, an outcropping that would prove very valuable as they mixed it to create mortar.

"If we build a saw pit, we can start cutting boards for the barracks," one of the men mentioned. There were whip saws in the supplies Mel had ordered.

Cutting wood in a saw pit soon became the least desirable of the jobs. Mel took a turn standing under the wood they were cutting, and she got dust in the collar of her shirt, in her hair, and in her pants. It was horrible! The days were hot, and the sweat made everything itch. She longed to whip off her shirt and jump in the creek like the men.

"If we block the creek up there," another man mentioned, "we would create a little pond down here, and that would be good for the animals." He didn't mention that it would look nice too, but Mel thought it looked wonderful as they proceeded with his suggestion. She went out there one night, creeping down into the valley well after the men were asleep to bathe and get the dust out of her pores. She didn't dare remove her bindings but managed to feel much better for it as she changed into clean clothes and washed the dust-filled clothes.

"It's your turn!" one of the stockmen told another the next day, demanding that he go down in the pit and use the saws. The boards were building up, and the barracks building was nearly complete. Mel wanted the roof in slate, and one of the men knew how to install that using whatever flat rocks could be found. It became a game for people to hunt for and find the flat rocks. The rocks were drilled through on

one end and nails were pounded through them into the wood roof, further protecting the building from the elements.

"I ain't going to do it. I can't stand the dust up my nose, and my eyes itched for three days last time. I'll herd sheep, I'll cut down trees and build, but I won't go in that saw pit, and you can't make me!" the man protested.

"I'll make you…" the other man started, but Mel was there by that time, having heard the ruction.

"You agreed to work for me. That means you will do any jobs given to you on this place. If you won't do your fair share, then you won't work for me," she told him, getting between him and the other stockman.

"You don't own all this," he gestured to the raw land around them, the piles of trees and wood boards building up, the building they were working on, and the fences taking shape. Two of the men were marking out additional buildings that Mel wanted for a shearing shed, a couple barns, and a chicken coop. "You just came out here and claimed all this. Who are you to order me about?" he asked belligerently.

"I thought I was your employer. You agreed to the conditions I laid out to everyone. You don't like it, then make your way back to Wilcannia."

"You'd put me off like that? After all the work I did helping you get here?"

"You agreed to work for me. I told you all it was new and raw. I said there would be plenty of work but there would also be plenty of food, and you agreed to work for me. If you're not willing to do the work, you aren't staying on my place." She leaned in, daring him to take a swing at her and knowing it would hurt because he was as big as she. She watched every move he made, hoping to duck in time when he finally made his move.

"What about my pay?" he asked, sounding angrier than Mel had guessed he could be.

"I've got it, and I'll give you supplies for two weeks, enough to get you back to Wilcannia."

"You'd turn me into a swagman? There's other jobs I could do besides that," he gestured at the pit where the men in it were staring up, aghast at the way he was speaking to the owner.

"You're turning yourself into a swagman. You agreed to work, and you aren't doing your fair share. Gather your gear, and I'll have your supplies and pay readied." She knew a swagman was a traveler who went from station to station, sometimes helping with little tasks or even fighting fires, earning enough for food and supplies. Other times, they just traveled from station to station, basically asking for a handout. She'd been surprised how many people put up with that, but it was some sort of code out here in the Outback.

The man turned away disgusted but not before mumbling, "I'd rather not work for a coon lover anyway."

"What did you say?" Mel roared.

He turned back, finally finding the fight he had been looking for. "I said I wouldn't want to work for a coon lover," he gestured towards Alinta.

Mel didn't wait. Her fist was coming up to strike the man in his big mouth just as her father had shown her so long ago, but she so rarely

used. She'd made sure her thumb was not in the way, so it wouldn't get broken. Girls did that, and Mel hadn't behaved like a girl in a long time. It felt good when her blow struck home, and she followed it up with a left to the man's gut as his back arched from the blow to his mouth. As he bent over to take the blow to his stomach, her knee was lifting, and his head was thrown back when the knee bone hit his nose. He went down. Mel was tempted to use her boots on him, but instead, she wiped the back of her hand across her mouth. She was breathing hard. "You get off my station! The rest of you take that as a warning," she glanced around at the men staring at the fight caused by the man's insubordination. "My wife is not to be disparaged in any way. I ever hear you saying anything like that again, and I'll kill you."

The man looked up fearfully. It had happened so quickly, and he hadn't been prepared. He was tempted to continue the fight, but the look in Mel's dark brown eyes told him the man would kill him. Had he known it was really a woman, he would have been so humiliated he would have been forced to fight back. He nodded, one hard nod, and he gingerly felt his jaw and broken nose, the blood running down his mouth and chin.

"Half an hour. Roll your swag, and I'll have your pay ready, so you can get out of here," Mel told him with finality. Then, she looked up at the staring men. "Get back to work. Any of you feel the same way he does, come see me, and I'll give you your pay and enough supplies to get back to Wilcannia." Mel turned to go where the supplies were stacked neatly under tarps and began measuring out what she had promised the man.

"I'm gonna be going with me mate," a voice said tentatively as she measured. She glanced up to see who it was, nodded once, and doubled the portions she was pouring into bags. By the time she was done, the two men had gathered their rolls, their hats, and their coats, and Mel handed them the bag of supplies with their pay. She watched as they began to make their way to the southeast, towards where the men had begun cutting a trail through the trees and brush and where eventually. she would cut a track to be connected to civilization.

Mel washed her knuckles in a cold bucket of water, shaking now that the men were gone and the confrontation was over. Alinta watched her carefully. She had never witnessed such violence between two human beings. She had seen what had happened when she was captured but had thought that an isolated incident. The violence frightened her, and she hadn't understood all the words. That night as they lay in their hut, Alinta asked, "What is coon lover?"

Mel could feel the anger and disgust she had felt earlier building up again. "You don't need–" she began but realized that wasn't fair. Alinta didn't know how cruel the white man could be, and then she rethought that as Ainia began suckling. Alinta did indeed know how cruel the white man could be, and this innocent child was the result of that rape. "He was referring to the color of your skin. Some men think darker skin means you are less human than they are. The word coon refers to someone with darker skin. It is not a kind word."

Alinta didn't know if she should be upset by that expression but thought perhaps Mel had already taken care of it for her. She didn't understand the full connotations of the word. "There are those with darker skin than mine," she commented.

Mel nodded, wondering if aboriginal people came in different skin tones. She knew they certainly looked different, just as whites did. The ones she had seen at Twin Station had flatter noses than Alinta, who looked almost like a white woman with a dark tan. She remembered the negroes she had seen in New Orleans and how dark they had been. Theirs were nothing like the skin tones she had seen here in Australia. It had bothered her that America still practiced slavery, especially after she had come from England where they had abolished it. She didn't think anyone should own another human being. "I think I have the prettiest wife," she murmured, watching and smiling as Alinta fed Ainia.

"Pretty is like flower?" Alinta asked, to be sure of the meaning of the word. Mel had picked her flowers one day, but she had misunderstood and thought they were to eat. She shredded them but found no food value and Mel had been forced to explain.

"Or like a sunrise or sunset," Mel explained, pleased to get off the subject of the men and their foul mouths. She hoped nothing would happen to the men in their travels and cause them to seek vengeance. She knew the other men were talking about the fight she had won. She thought about that. Did anyone ever really win a fight?

CHAPTER THREE

Mel split up her men. Those who were staying on at the home station continued to build the outbuildings, although the size and dimensions of her house were already laid out. The basement had been dug, lined with rocks, and a sturdy foundation rose above the grounds. Sleeper beams—big, heavy logs—had been rolled into place along the tops of the foundation and boards placed across them for the first floor. The rest would wait for the Irishman and his crew as the men continued to gather wood for the buildings. Meanwhile, some of the men helped her clear the track she was going to build to her other fold that had been built, other prime locations they would find, and on towards Wilcannia. She hoped they wouldn't have to go too far beyond where she estimated the station line was, where the odd domed hills between Twin Station and Lawrence Station were located. She wanted to find a

track already built, but she was willing to go all the way back to Wilcannia to build her own track if it was necessary. They needed to open this route, so she could get necessary supplies. In the months since she had left Twin Station, she was sure a flurry of activity was going on as a result of the letters she had posted. She wanted to be ready when the stock, supplies, and people she anticipated would eventually come down the track. It would be foolish for anyone to have to go all the way to Twin Station to find her track into their station. It was so far south and out of the way.

Mother Nature was thorough, and she was fast. Already, this fold she had built had been growing wild. The bushes she had relocated had been intertwining with the wood she had laid all around it to form fenced walls. The creek near it made for a beautiful and scenic spot, and she had enjoyed grazing her sheep here. Already, a couple men had taken pack horses and gone to resupply her stockmen, who were tending her sheep down the other track. She'd instructed her solicitor and accountant to purchase more sheep for her, and she hoped they'd be coming down the track eventually. As they continued through the plains, meadows, and up around hills, she hoped they were choosing the best spots for the track that wound through the land. They saw no sign of the two men who had left the station, but she wished them no ill will and hoped they had made it to another station, perhaps to Wilcannia or even farther.

The trees they felled that could be used were hauled back along the track, the drag making a further impression on the virgin land and solidifying the track they were building.

They had been gone weeks from the home paddock when they finally spotted another track. Having no idea where it went, they rode their horses down it and onto another station where they met the owner late the next day. He was expecting them as he had spotted their dust. This proved to Mel that Fabiola was mistaken about there being no one north of her, although they were much farther east than she expected to find anyone.

"Are you lost?" he asked heartily, surprised to see the men coming from west of his place.

"No, we were building a track and came across this one," Mel told him, indicating the one they were now following. "We may be neighbors," she said in a friendly voice. "I'm Mel Lawrence."

"Neighbors?" he asked, surprised. His eyebrows disappeared into his hairline and under his bangs that the wind was whipping across his forehead. "I have no neighbors for miles in any direction."

"We've taken up a place north of Twin Station," Mel informed him warily, worried that he would resent her presence. She knew men like this, who thought they were kings in their own fiefdoms.

"I hadn't heard of anyone in the vicinity. Welcome, Yank," he said, holding out his hand, which Mel took, pleased he wasn't upset. "I'm Harris Covington. You have family?"

"Yes, my wife and daughter are back at the home paddock," she informed him. "You?"

The man nodded proudly. "I have two boys and my wife, although I may have to send her back to Sydney. Some can't stand the Outback," he said, lowering his voice almost apologetically.

Mel nodded sagely. Pointing, she asked, "Does this track lead to your station or go across it?"

"This one goes across it but takes a southeastern bent and goes on to a few other stations before hitting some of the smaller towns out here and then eventually, Wilcannia."

"I have men, animals, and supplies coming in. Will there be any trouble with any of the stations if they use this track?" she asked as they began to walk their horses, the men listening avidly.

They walked and talked for a ways, the man pointing out where the track split. "If you go that way, you'll come to my home station…eventually." He pointed east and north, the way the track wound around into the distance. Things were far apart out here, and they all knew it. "It was a pleasure to meet you, Mel Lawrence," he said as he shook her hand again. "If you have the time, you should come for a visit. My Audrey would like to meet your wife."

"Maybe when we have our house built, you would like to come for a visit out at our place too and see those Merino sheep I told you about."

"I'd like that," Harris replied as he saluted and rode off, stopping to wave from a hill on the track before disappearing over the other side.

"Nice enough bloke," one of the men commented, and Mel nodded. Their discussion had gone from what in the world was an American doing in the middle of Australia, or rather the far reaches of New South Wales, to the different breeds of cattle, horses, and especially sheep. Harris was very interested that she had managed to purchase so many Merinos and wanted to hear the story of where she got them and her own trek out here onto the Outback with the niece of the former owner

of Twin Station. Mel knew that the gossip and stories the man would share would feed him, his men, and even his wife and children for years.

They continued down the track, and it took days moving at a brisk pace before they saw signs of civilization. Mel was pleased when the track did indeed take them to Wilcannia. She stopped at the post office for her mail, introducing herself to the postmaster and making herself known. She explained about the track they had just opened to Lawrence Station. She knew that word of the new track would spread and those seeking the station wouldn't have to go so far out of their way to reach them via Twin Station. Now, they only had to go as far north and west as her track. She purchased some white paint, several posts, and flat, narrow sheets of wood, tying everything up behind her horse. She bought some supplies, noting the higher prices out here due to its remoteness and the fact they had to haul everything in. She looked out at the Cobdogla River for a time, knowing if she followed it south it would eventually take her to Menindee. It had been renamed the Darling River, but it was distinctive for being probably the muddiest river she had ever seen. She recalled being told it was the only river in the world that flowed upside down, and she believed it. The silt in it made it very murky.

Mel gave the men that were returning with her two days to blow off steam in the town as she gathered her few things. She didn't find too much she wanted in the remote town, and she was hoping by some miracle that some of the supplies or animals she had purchased would roll into town while they were there. They didn't, of course. It was too soon, and she and the men that hadn't been paid off headed back to the station and the enormous amount of work waiting for them there. At night beside the fire, Mel painted several signs, using her knife to shape one end into a point, which would point the way to Lawrence Station where the track forked. As they traveled, she pounded the posts in deep, hoping neither the weather nor any malicious persons would take the signs down. She wanted the drovers and the carters, or teamsters as she would have called them, to be able to find her station. It was far too easy to get lost out here, and she couldn't afford to run out of supplies.

CHAPTER FOUR

Alinta hadn't liked the fact that she would be left alone with all the men working at the home station, so Mel had tried to introduce her to the women married to the stockmen she had hired. Their houses would be built next, and Mel had asked the men to prepare the sites. They chose the areas near a creek and down the hill from where the main house would go. They were also well away from the barns and paddocks. It was a nice site, shaded by the immense trees, and the houses would be on stilts in case the creek flooded. They had decided not to put in foundations like the main house and barns since the debris could build up if it did flood. The lumber was readily available, and while the men were not builders, they were piling up the wood they had sawed in preparation for construction. Meanwhile, the weather had held, and it wasn't cold yet. Summer was waning though, and a couple of the wives were getting anxious. They didn't like living in tents and huts.

The women were cautiously friendly with the aboriginal woman, aware that she was the wife of the owner. The men were respectful, not daring to say anything cross around her. The fight with the banished worker was still fresh in their minds, and they knew if they crossed Mel Lawrence they might be on the bad end of his fists. The women and Alinta decided to put in a garden. This was a new concept to the aboriginal gatherer and scavenger, but as the women explained the concept, she became enthused. The thought that she wouldn't have to go far afield and could grow her own plants and vegetables greatly appealed to her. A couple of the men and the women helped dig up for a large garden on a flat space that they could easily water from the creek, turning over the soil repeatedly before planting some of the seeds Mel had brought. Many of the seeds and plants were unfamiliar to Alinta, but she nodded as the women tried to explain them to her, and she learned new words and tried to picture in her head what they were describing. The women were cautiously kind to the native woman. They knew she had the owner's ear, and they didn't know if she was the type who would complain to Mel if they were unkind. Their husbands' livelihoods depended on this station, and so far, Mel had been a good and fair employer.

Ainia hung in the wrap Alinta had made, never far from her mother's heartbeat as the woman worked. The other women, even one who had a young son of her own, cooed over the baby. For the first time, Alinta felt as though she belonged, and it was an odd feeling. Their people remained respectful, but they also shared things with her,

although not everything they would have normally shared with their contemporaries. They took pride in their little community and explored the immediate vicinity around the home paddocks.

One of the men returned from taking supplies out to the stockmen. He was leading a stockman's horse with the man on it. The stockman's leg was a pulpy mess as he had been gored by a wild boar. Another stockman drew supplies and immediately set out to cover the man's fold. His sheep had been left with only a jackaroo to tend the flock. Alinta got to work on the injured man, using wild plants she had gathered to cleanse the wound, spiderwebs to stop the bleeding, and a sewing needle Mel had given her to practice on clothing to sew the wound shut. She made the man get up and walk on the damaged leg twice a day as it healed, using a stout stick for support, and he didn't like her for that. The other men warned him not to say anything, telling of the fight and the subsequent firing of the man who had left, but he already knew the story. The men who delivered his supplies had left out nothing in the telling. He was careful what he said to the aboriginal woman despite her nagging him to walk. She tried to explain he would heal faster if he was up and about, and she had found him a forked branch to hobble around on. He knew he was lucky to be alive. Wild boars were vicious, and it would have killed him if the dogs hadn't distracted the animal while he'd gotten off a shot, hitting just behind the ear of the beast.

Mel returned after weeks away, pleased to see her wife and happy with the progress the men had made on the place while she was gone. They'd dragged a few trees from down the track they had built, and

now, Mel and her men brought others behind their own horses to add to the large pile.

"How are you doing?" she asked the stockman when she learned of his goring by the wild boar.

"Fair to middling. Your missus has been looking after me."

"I heard," she said, amused and waiting for the man to say something, yet hoping he wasn't too angry after hearing what the other stockmen and her wife had told her.

"You know, she's a bit of nag," he began and saw Mel stiffen, "but she was right. It's healin' fair to dinkum fast." He grinned to show he didn't hold any ill will towards Alinta.

Mel grinned, nodding. "She'll have you in good shape in no time."

"Will I get my place back?" he fretted.

"You want to go back?"

"Aye, I kind of like the place, and if you'll help me write a letter, I'd like to send for my missus to come out with the supply train."

"I'll do that," Mel promised. Now that the track was open to Wilcannia, they could send a rider there periodically for the mail. Some of the men needed to blow off steam sometimes, and she was certain someone would be willing to go when she was ready to send off some more correspondence.

When the time came, Mel had no need to bother sending off her own men. As she was working on the fence in the hidden valley, which she would use to keep her stock close to home once they arrived, she was hailed from above. Shading her eyes, she saw one of her men waving to her and calling. She put down the axe she had used to split some rails, and one of her men picked it up. She made her way to her horse, saddled it, and mounted up. There was a pretty good trail up the side of the valley, which led up to the spot where the house would go. The foundation was laid, the first floor was already down and solid, and Mel rode on past it to where the barns and corrals were laid out, ending next to the barracks, the only finished structure.

"There's cattle and such coming on down the track," the man pointed as she stopped at a corral. Mel looked from her vantage point on the hill to see the dust roiling up from the track they had built.

"Has anyone spotted the animals, or are we maybe just getting visitors?" she asked, removing her hat to wipe at her forehead with the sleeve from her shirt. Her hair was tied back with a bandana.

"I saw them and came to warn you. I was hauling logs from the path on that section about two miles along there," he pointed with his chin.

Mel nodded, getting down from her horse and tying him off. Someone had knocked together a trough that held water. It wasn't well done and leaked, but at least the horse could drink. She glanced at the skies, wondering at the clouds moving in. She knew they were heading towards fall and winter and the many storms that would come with those seasons. Already, they had gotten a few small squalls but nothing major yet. She looked towards the track that came in from the west, the one they had built to get in here originally and connect her folds to Twin Station. She wondered if Shamus O'Grady had decided not to come and build her house after all. She would be very disappointed if he didn't show up. The supplies and animals she was expecting, the ones coming in from the track they had built to Wilcannia, would contain some of the things Shamus had said they would need from

Sydney. She had expected to work around those things as they built her house. She glanced at the hut her wife was living in, oblivious to the fact that their men lived better under a real roof in the barracks. She glanced to the tents they had set up for those stockmen with women and children, deciding they needed homes for all these people first.

"Have a few men ready to help when they get past the creek," she ordered, and the man ran off to comply.

Mel considered taking the saddle off her horse again but decided against it. She might need it, and she wasn't certain what animals were coming down the track. She looked again to where she could see the visible dust cloud. It was then, she noticed there seemed to be a second dust cloud on the other track too. She frowned as she looked and looked again. Certain she was seeing things but hopeful they would come too, she continued to stare at it. The dust smudge on the horizon wasn't conclusive.

"Visitors?" Alinta asked as she came up. Mel put her arm around her wife, hugging her close. She was longing for more but unable to do anything about it. She wanted a home for her wife, and she hoped to build it for her soon, so they could be alone together…just them and Ainia. She was overly concerned that someone would observe them and figure out that Mel was a woman.

"Yes, Dan said he saw them himself when he was hauling trees," she said, mentioning the stockman who had run to gather others to help.

Alinta smiled. The name Dan meant something entirely different in her language, and she still found these white names hard to say sometimes. Fortunately, this one was easy.

"Do you see dust over that way?" Mel pointed with her chin towards the other track that came in from the south. Heading over the far side of the hills, it led off towards the folds in that direction and eventually, Twin Station. She thought perhaps it was wishful thinking on her part but trusted her wife's eyesight implicitly. She had spotted animals in the brush far sooner than Mel could, even when they were camouflaged. Alinta thought nothing of it, amazed that Mel didn't see what seemed so obvious to her.

"Yes. More visitors?"

"I'm hoping it's Shamus O'Grady come to build our house and barns."

"What if he don't come?"

"If he doesn't come?" Mel corrected automatically, shrugging philosophically. "Then, I guess we can make do with building on our own, but I'd rather have someone who knows what they are doing build them with the help of our manpower." She wondered if her wife understood all that.

"You build bunk," she stated, pointing with her own chin at the barracks the men had built. A trail of smoke was rising from the chimney that climbed up the center of the building and kept it warm and toasty for the men.

"The bunkhouse…er, barracks," she corrected, "isn't a hard building to put up, but the house, the barns, and the sheds are important for the future of the station."

They watched the dust clouds as they came closer. The one to the south was becoming more visible, and the dust cloud to the southeast appeared much, much larger. Mel surmised that one of the dust clouds contained the animals she had sent for. The sheep folds here at the home station were ready and could hold thousands of animals. The corrals were for horses and cows, and the pens were for pigs. The pens hadn't been hard to build, and the men were able to put those together for Mel. They'd run out of nails in their building efforts, and Mel had been about ready to send someone from the station to buy a keg or two in Wilcannia and take the mail with them at the same time. She wanted to go herself but didn't want to leave her wife right before the rainy season, which was almost upon them. She looked out at the countryside, amazed that no one else lived in this vast interior. It was dry, but she was certain the area next to the hidden valley where she had decided to build her home was paradise. The beauty and splendor of the place intrigued her daily. She really enjoyed her almost nightly walks with her wife and daughter. Occasionally, they rode horses and explored north of the chosen homesite. Mel had plans for paddocks and folds up there as her flocks grew.

As the larger cloud drew closer, Mel could see the distant figures coming over the hills. Then, she saw the reason for the enormous cloud of dust rising over the trees and hills. It was being created by the row of carts she saw first. There were many, many carts followed by thousands of hoofs churning the grasses to dust. The track had been well worn from the trees they had dragged for their building efforts and now, it was flattened and compacted beyond anything Mel could have hoped to do herself. In many places the track had begun to grow, and nature was reclaiming it with plants that had sporadically sprung up down the center between the paths of the wheels, but now, those plants were trampled into nothingness as the animals came and continued to

come. No wonder it had taken them so long to arrive. It must have taken an extensive amount of time for her solicitor to find someone he could trust with the large order Mel had sent him, much less to find and purchase the animals and arrange to have them driven onto the far Outback.

Mel let go of her wife, kissing her before mounting up on the back of her horse. She didn't rush, but she headed down the hill and skirted the playing puppies. She had been relieved that all the puppies the two bitches had birthed had shown an interest in sheep. She'd pulled half a dozen sheep from one of the nearest folds just to test the pups. She kept the few wethers at the home paddocks for their personal consumption and now, she was using them to train the pups as they grew. One of the pups had been borderline, and Mel had worried that she would have to destroy him. It turned out it had just taken a little longer for him to realize what his siblings instinctively knew; the sheep were to be herded.

Several men mounted their own horses and followed Mel as she went to meet the drovers. Passing those on the long line of carts pulled by bullocks, she lifted her hat a few times as she saw women in the carts, nodding to the drivers as she headed for the animals that were being driven onto her station. She couldn't see the end of the massive flock, which was bigger than the one she had helped birth on this very station. They were crowded down the track, spreading out only when they came to open meadows and grass. The dogs and the drovers were having a time of it, but that was the nature of herding. Fortunately, sheep tended to follow their leaders, usually a ram, but often, they would follow a sheep if the drover tied a bell around its neck. That was

where the term bellwether came from. They would follow the sound of the bell or the strong leader. A couple riders separated themselves from the flock, riding wide around it to avoid startling the sheep as they trotted their horses towards the group approaching them.

"I'm looking for Miss Lawrence?" the man in front asked, his Cockney accent sounding thick to Mel.

"I'm Mel Lawrence," she said by way of introduction.

The man flushed, evidently expecting a woman based on the instructions given to him back in Sydney by the solicitor. The man touched his hat to acknowledge the station owner, sure the mistake had been his own. It had been a long trip, and he was exhausted. He couldn't wait to turn around and head back, but he had been paid well to perform this duty, and he was glad to see he was nearing the end of his job. "I'm Braun," he said by way of introduction. "I have this for you," he added, reaching into his saddle bag and extracting a packet of letters. "Those are from Mr. Saunders," he said, handing her the bound pack of paperwork from her solicitor. Next, he reached in the other saddlebag and pulled out a larger packet, "I also stopped in Wilcannia for your mail."

Mel nodded, taking both packets in her hands as she looked at the man, wondering if he would ask where *Miss* Lawrence was. It was obvious he was a little confused but had accepted Mel Lawrence as a man. "How was the trip?" she asked to distract him as she stuffed the wrapped packets into her own saddlebags, curious as the sheep were coming closer. She walked her horse to the side, so they could pass by and she could observe them. "Go lend a hand and get them in the folds," she said to the men who had accompanied her and then, she glanced at the other men. The men who had accompanied Braun, curious about the station owner, touched their fingertips to their hats in an odd little salute before riding away to help her men with the animals.

"Long," Braun admitted. "I'd never been this far out, but your solicitor offered me a good deal. I'm sure the details are in a letter in that," he nodded to the packet she was stuffing in the bag.

Mel nodded in agreement as she straightened up. "Many losses?"

"A few, mostly stragglers that the dingoes got, but a few ate something they shouldn't have at a billabong and snakes bit a couple."

Mel had expected losses. It was not much different from her experience herding the Merinos on her own trip. It seemed so long ago. Was it only eighteen months or so ago? No, it had to be longer than that. She'd have to check her calendar. "What kind of sheep did you manage to bring me?" was her next question, knowing that finding those Merinos had been a once in a lifetime deal, and unless she was willing to send to England for purebreds, she might never find them again. Still, mixing them with these breeds she saw coming down the track would give them good meat and wool sheep.

He began to tell her about the Leicester sheep he had found for her. They looked odd with their shorn coats that had started to grow in on the trip. Their long ears made them look like odd-shaped, miniature versions of llamas, based on pictures Mel had seen of those animals. The Poll Dorset and the White Suffolk sheep they had obtained for her were more common, and they were the types of sheep most people expected to see. From having talked with Foster and other grazers, she knew a few of the breeds on sight and by description. She could see that a lot of interbreeding had been going on here in Australia. The

Leicester would be good for wool production, the Poll Dorset and the White Suffolk for meat, but the Merinos were good for both, so blending all these breeds would be profitable. She watched as the sheep began to stream by them and continued to talk with Braun.

They discussed the track leading into the station. He was appreciative of the signs she had posted, laughing that no one had thought of doing this before based on what a few of his men, who had traveled in the Outback, had told him. "I'm sure it will catch on as they spread the word," he said with a laugh.

Mel laughed with him and asked about the cattle, the pigs, the poultry, and the horses she had also ordered. They carried on with their conversation as the sheep continued to stream by and finally, the cattle, pigs, and a large herd of horses brought up the rear. She eyed them appreciatively, seeing one or two that she was wanted to take a closer look at. She felt that a couple might possibly compare to Carmen's fine steeds. The dust cloud overwhelmed them, and they both pulled handkerchiefs up to cover their mouths and noses as they followed the long line of animals. It must have been quite a feat getting all these animals, and Mel wondered if the poultry she had ordered was in some of the carts and she had just missed them. The carts had been piled high with bags, barrels, boxes, and other supplies she had ordered, and she hadn't taken the time to look too closely.

"There's room in the barracks for a few of your men and yourself. Come up and meet my missus when you've had a chance to settle in. I'll send down some rum for you and your men," she promised, and Braun thanked her on their behalf as they went their separate ways at the bottom of the hill where he headed off to the only finished building.

Men were busy parking the many carts alongside the paddocks, and they were herding sheep, cows, horses, and pigs into the various paddocks and pens. Mel headed for the other track, skirting around the large garden her wife and the stockmen's wives had started while she was gone. The garden was flourishing, and someone had made a wheel of sorts that pumped water and allowed the entire garden to be watered from the creek. As a result, the garden looked good despite the end-of-summer heat.

Riding up the southern track a ways, Mel saw the source of the second dust cloud. She smiled when she recognized Carmen and Fabiola, and she was surprised to see Harold traveling with them as well. She smiled again when she saw Shamus O'Grady and his men, their tools piled high in the cart they were riding in. He returned her wave a bit too enthusiastically, and he toppled over in the cart. His men helped to prop him back up.

"He's been drinking a wee bit," Carmen laughed as she came up, sounding like she was speaking with O'Grady's Irish brogue. It was funny to hear the Hispanic-Californian trying to imitate an Irish brogue and they all smiled at her attempt.

"Hello. It's nice to see you both," she said by way of greeting. Harold's eyes bored into hers until she amended her greeting to include him. "This is a surprise. I was only expecting Shamus and some of his men."

"We had to make sure he got here," Fabiola told her, disgusted by how much rum the man imbibed while complaining the whole time that it wasn't good Irish whiskey.

"But aren't you busy at your own station?" Mel asked, concerned that this trip had taken them away from their work. She knew how much work there was year-round to run a station.

"It'll still be there when we return," Fabiola told her, a look of determination in her eye. "I was curious about what you are building here," she admitted, a slight smile on her face.

Mel was startled. This was the first time she had felt a friendly vibe from the prickly Australian. She smiled in return. "Well, we aren't far along, and I'm really glad to see Shamus and his men. We have the boards and some other things waiting for him, and we just got in more men and supplies."

"That can't possibly be the cloud we saw," Harold put in, sounding almost sulky or envious.

Mel nodded her head as she turned to follow them down the track towards the home paddock. She had noted there seemed to be a couple more carts. The Aborigines in them were of all ages, and they were looking curiously at her. Fabiola noticed her perusal of them.

"You did say they were welcome to build a village and work here, didn't you?"

"Yes, I'm very glad they are here. There's so much work to do and so much to build!" She turned to address Harold's query. "I ordered stock from Sydney, and it finally got here. There are sheep, cattle, and even horses," she added as she looked towards Carmen. "I think you'll see one or two that might get Dancer's attention," she said with a nod towards the stallion the Hispanic woman was riding so expertly. "Hello, Paco," she said to the ever-present vaquero that followed a few paces behind his mistress.

"Senor Lawrence," he nodded in greeting, pleased to see the American. He understood now that there was only a good friendship between his mistress and the Yankee. He had been suspicious of his intentions when Mel first made Carmen's acquaintance back in Sydney.

"I was worried that something happened on your place to delay the building of your hacienda," Mel commented, hinting about the long delay in seeing Shamus O'Grady arrive. She had expected him weeks ago, even months ago at the rate he had been building.

"He built us some fine barns, and with the help of my vaqueros and the stockmen the home paddock is transformed," Carmen admitted.

Mel caught the prideful look on her friend's face, and she almost missed the tender look on Fabiola's face as she looked at Carmen. It was almost a look of adoration. This shocked Mel entirely, and she didn't miss the annoyed look on Harold's face, and she wondered at that.

They rode companionably along on the track, discussing the needs of a home station as they came upon the slowly transforming hillside and all the work Mel's men had accomplished.

"You do not plan small, my friend," Carmen understated, seeing the dimensions of the barns and sheds she had laid out. The stone foundations were arranged and waiting for the builders, and the sleepers were already mounted on them. Enormous stacks of cut board also lay in neat piles at the various building sites, covered with tarps to protect them from the impending rains.

"Not at all. I plan to have a large operation, maybe as large as your own place including your southern paddocks," she teased Fabiola gently, reminding her of their determination to have her settle south of

them instead of north. From what she had heard, she was glad she hadn't chosen to go farther west. Apparently, it was bare desert out there, and while Alinta assured her they could survive, she admitted that the large number of beasts could not survive there since there was not enough grazing land farther west, much less enough water to support them all. Mel already knew many of the places she had chosen to put folds were sparse and couldn't support large flocks of sheep. That's why they were spaced far apart, and the stockmen were required to move them around the paddocks she was setting up. "I've planned for the flocks I intend to have."

"And you've brought in more sheep before you got your checks for the wool?" Harold asked, listening to her and looking about. There was a lot of activity as the men got the bullocks that had been hauling the long line of carts in order, and her other men settled the large mass of animals they had brought.

"Yes, I thought I might as well while I had the opportunity, and the prices were low," she exchanged a look with Carmen, who remembered their discussions about how much cheaper sheep were immediately after they had been shorn. "I am going to crossbreed them with my Merinos, and hopefully, we will get more wool." They hadn't gotten the checks from their wool yet because it had been shipped to England. She hoped one of the letters in her saddlebags would inform her that the wool had either been shipped or that it had arrived.

Their conversation flowed easily, and they pulled up near the corrals. They took the saddles off their mounts, and two of Mel's men came to take the horses from them. They left the saddles on the fence since Mel hadn't built a tack room yet. Shamus O'Grady and his men stopped their cart near the barracks and got out unsteadily. Two men quickly unhitched the bullocks from the cart. The Aborigines stood around once they got out of their own cart and looked about. Alinta came up, pleased to see Carmen and greeting her enthusiastically.

"Oh, let me see that baby," the woman said and held out her arms for the darling girl.

Alinta happily gave their friend the baby, who studied the dark-haired woman with her baby blue eyes. Ainia's eye hadn't turned dark like Alinta's own, and their brightness fascinated the aboriginal woman; she likened them to the sky.

"It's good to see you," Fabiola told her, smiling, and a surprised Alinta returned the smile. Harold nodded to her before walking off towards where the men were congregating. Already, boisterous laughter was coming from the barracks. "Whatever you do, don't let Shamus find your rum," she warned Mel quietly.

Mel turned to her, alarmed. "I was going to send some rum down for Braun and his men to celebrate the end of their long drive. They brought all these animals," her hands gestured, taking in the full folds and paddocks and the many animals already getting used to their new accommodations and settling down. Many of the animals were eating the overgrown grasses that had continued to grow despite the fences Mel and her men had put up.

Carmen came up, cuddling the baby and bouncing her a little. "We came with him to see you both," her smile took in both Mel and Alinta, "but also to make sure he got here in one piece. It took him much longer to build what we wanted because he and his men found our rum supply. They were drunk half the time. For God's sake, keep your rum under lock and key."

Mel nodded, wanting to laugh but knowing it really wasn't funny. There was a lot of work that had to be done, and the man had delayed it by months due to his drinking. "I'll bet there's rum in those supplies," she said, nodding to the many carts that had come in from the southeast and were now parked against the many corrals and sheep folds in a long but neat row.

"Lock it up," Fabiola stated, repeating Carmen's warning. She was not amused. The man had nearly caused a fire with his carelessness, but when he was sober, he was one of the hardest working men she had ever known. The hacienda he had built for Carmen was beautiful. The barns were first class, but they had taken much too long to build.

"Why they here?" Alinta pointed at the aboriginal people standing about and looking lost.

"I told them they could come here and there would be jobs if they wanted to live here. Is that okay?" Mel asked, suddenly concerned that her wife wouldn't want them here. They weren't her people, and she hadn't been able to communicate with them when they were on Twin Station.

"Oh, most of them aren't from our station," Fabiola told her, much to Mel's surprise. "Word spread, and they came with us when we decided to escort Shamus here."

"How did they know when you were leaving?" Mel asked, confused as to how word had gotten about.

Fabiola shrugged and answered, "If you can tell me how they know things half the time, we will both have learned something. They are mysterious and at one with this land."

Mel nodded, wondering how they had heard, but Alinta had told her that an Aborigine could send messages over long distances and that word would spread if they wanted it. Mel didn't quite understand it, but she was certain her wife didn't understand a lot of what she tried to explain about white people either. Mel was still looking at Alinta, concerned that she didn't want those people to live here on the station, and waiting on her answer.

"Yes, okay," Alinta said, sounding odd as she looked at the dozen or so people standing there watching the white people interact. She glanced at the white women, who appeared to be a little uncomfortable as they looked about the unfinished place. They were clustered together, almost as if for protection it looked like.

"Why don't we go and introduce ourselves?" Mel asked jovially, directing her question to Carmen, Fabiola, and Alinta. "You can put your things down by our fire," she pointed to where Alinta had obviously started their dinner. She saw there was more food than usual by the fire. Her wife must have known they would have guests.

"I'll go with you," Fabiola volunteered, and Carmen came along as they walked towards the group of Aborigines.

"This is Mister Lawrence," Fabiola enunciated slowly, "and her wife, Missus Lawrence."

Their eyes, especially the adults' eyes opened wide. They saw that Alinta was full-blood Aborigine but not of their tribe.

"Welcome. Thank you for coming. We can build you some houses along the creek," Mel began, but one of the elders made a sideways motion with his hand that Mel caught. Being around Alinta, she was much more aware of these things than she had been before.

"We build huts," he said in pidgin English.

"No, I would like you to have houses," she contradicted.

"Mel, they are fine in–" Fabiola began.

"I've seen their huts. Their huts are fine if they are living in the bush. I would like them to have nice homes built of wood," she insisted. She had given this a lot of thought. She had asked Alinta if people like her own tribe or other tribes would like wood houses, and she hadn't been sure.

"Our huts fine," the man insisted.

"Yes, they are. Why don't we build both for your people to choose?" she offered, and he smiled as he nodded. "Would you like to build them there?" she pointed along the creek, well away from where she would be building the stockmen's houses, so the Aborigines' village had privacy. She knew some people would be prejudiced against these natives, regardless of how hard they worked. "Do you need anything now?"

"Some tucker would probably go down good," Fabiola murmured helpfully.

"I'll send my men down with some food for you and your people," Mel offered, and the elder smiled appreciatively. "We can talk more after you get settled."

They watched as the group walked off in the direction Mel had indicated.

"You are going to have to be firm with them," Fabiola told her, mindful that Alinta was standing there and not wishing to insult their friend's wife. "A lot of Aborigines don't understand the concept of ownership. Have the men hunt dingoes and build things, but I've never seen a stockman who wasn't mixed. They just don't understand that the sheep aren't theirs to give away. Have the women work in the gardens or train their girls to watch Ainia," she advised, smiling at Carmen, who was still holding the little bundle.

Remembering that Fabiola and Harold's mother had been an Aborigine, Mel was surprised. "I'm sure they can learn if they want–" Mel began but was amazed when Alinta disagreed with her.

"Some won't learn. Won't give up old ways. They want to keep *their* ways. They take your tucker. Hunt dingoes. Won't live in house."

Mel smiled at her wife and shrugged. "Well, all we can do is try," she promised and then went to welcome the stockmen's wives who were also looking about, lost. "Hello, I'm Mel Lawrence, and this is my wife, Alinta…Missus Lawrence," she said by way of introduction, noticing a few eyes glaze over as they looked at her wife's brown skin. She filed that away for future reference. She wouldn't allow anyone to slight her wife; she was very proud of her. This was her place, their home, and her rules would be paramount. "We'll have houses up for the married stockmen in a few days. Meanwhile, you will have to make do as you did on the trek out here." Several agreed gracefully, but she could see a couple were annoyed that she wasn't ready for them and didn't have a place for them out of the weather. She noted it was the same women, who had been unable to mask their expressions while

being introduced to an aboriginal woman. She would remember that as well, expecting trouble at some point.

They enjoyed their evening of camaraderie around the fire, talking about the stock Mel had brought in. Braun joined them, talking knowledgeably, but he was anxious to head back to civilization as soon as possible. A couple of his drovers would be going back with him, but most had come to stay on, and Mel welcomed their presence. Already, her men were planning on dividing up the sheep and making new folds out in the bush, several on the track she had made towards the southeast. She knew of several places where she wanted to place them but only after the new, enormous workforce at the home station helped put up the barns, the stables, the sheds, and the house. She only hoped the rains would hold off long enough for them to accomplish at least some of what she was planning.

CHAPTER FIVE

The barns went up in record time. Mel was certain the amount of wood they had laid by contributed to its ease, but she also knew the sheer number of men working together helped raise the large structures. From the posts to the siding, using block and tackle helped the barns go up amazingly fast. O'Grady and his men were brilliant as they used the now firm and set foundations to place enormous sleepers using the block and tackle, which was much more effective than rolling those heavy beams at an angle onto the foundations like Mel and her men had done to place some of them. Stone floors went in several of the barns, while some were built with wood floors, and still others were left with the original dirt floors. The roofing was metal sheeting that had been shipped in the many carts. O'Grady put in dormers and gables on the second barn that would eventually match the main house he was

planning for Mel. It was called a Monitor style barn, and the house would look beautiful with this *modern* style. The first barn was of the Gambrel style, big, lofty, and with plenty of room for all their future needs.

The large shearing shed and the other sheds seemed like child's play to the men. They would have run out of siding, but O'Grady's men showed them how to make the whip saws much more efficient. They installed resourceful lighting in the shearing shed, so the shearers would be able to shear as long as daylight lasted and their backs held out. Several stockmen's houses went up by the creek on stilts as Mel had planned. They were shaded by the bountiful foliage of the trees, and each had a wide front porch, at least two bedrooms, a living room, and a kitchen to square off each house. There were also privies well away from the creek water, so they wouldn't contaminate the water. Each house had a wood stove as well as a fireplace and a bathtub, a convenience that none had thought of before, but Mel had been well prepared and planned carefully for them. The supplies had been carried in the many carts that had brought the workers out.

She knew the women could wash their clothes as well as their bodies in the tub, and it was a convenience she felt was necessary. She hoped it would help make those married stockmen and their wives content, so they would remain in this remote place.

A well was dug by the main house. It went down over forty feet because the house was on the side of the hill, but when it was done, the water was cool, fresh, delicious, and well worth the dangerous and arduous work. O'Grady knew how to hook the well water up to the house too. Once the walls were begun on the main house, he began

putting in piping, fashioning the pipes from the clay that was found in the valley. He coated thin trees with the raw clay, then burned away the wood using hot fires and creating clay pipes. They were able to have fresh water in the kitchen and in the two bathrooms the main house sported as well. A special stove with a reservoir pumped hot water into the bathtubs Mel had ordered. Windows made it all the way from Sydney with very little breakage as the glass was well cushioned in the carts. Replacement panels had been sent as well, just in case of damage, and they would store these for later use.

The stockmen's houses were only halfway built when Carmen and Fabiola insisted they must return to their own station. They had pitched in along with everyone else, and they too were amazed at the beautiful buildings that O'Grady had designed with Mel and how quickly they had gone up.

Mel thanked her friends and the men who had come with them for their help, then she and Alinta waved them on their way. Alinta would miss Carmen's help in caring for the small baby. She had doted on the little girl, who was growing like a weed. They'd given them well over a week of help, and Mel greatly appreciated it, but she knew they had as much work as she on their own station with the oncoming rainy season.

Mel asked O'Grady to put pipes in each of the stockmen's houses too, utilizing his technique to make the clay pipes and giving them fresh water from the tanks they installed under the shady trees. She wanted to do the same for the small aboriginal village that had gone up downstream, but Alinta vetoed that idea. She explained that too many white man conveniences might scare the natives off. Mel acquiesced

but still planned to put in small houses that she hoped they would eventually use, and these would have fresh water.

They were certain to finish the outside of the main house before the rains came with force. Mel quickly had the skeletons of the second floor put in place along with some of the inside support beams and room partitions. Some men were putting in the floor for the attics, some were finishing the siding, and some were already putting up the trusses for the various roofs that the house design called for. They'd already had a few small squalls—what the locals called brief showers—but knew that strong storms would hit this area of Australia, and they were racing against time to build the house. Even if they didn't get the inside rooms done, they had to get the siding up and the roof on. They could put shutters over the many windows Mel had ordered. The dormers, gables, and cupolas on the corners of the house meant lots of roof work for the men. Already, one man had fallen in a foolish accident and was recovering in one of the stockmen's houses.

Mel hadn't worked only on the buildings. She'd also had to sort the many animals and send one of the stockmen down the track with a flock, having him head towards the southeast and the one unoccupied fold she had built there. He took one thousand sheep with him, along with his dogs and a pack animal to carry his supplies. She was busy sorting the rest of the sheep as they couldn't support all these animals for an indefinite period at the home paddock. She sent many sheep down into the valley to graze on the luxuriant grasses that grew there. The pods of the various plants provided them with food, and the creek that ran through the valley enabled the men to water them twice a day.

The men hurried to finish the main house, and Mel moved into one corner of the kitchen with her wife and child just as the first real storm hit. The winds were terrible. They battered the house, but the family was snug and cozy with the fire as Mel taught Alinta how to use the stove and other fixtures she was unfamiliar with.

Alinta was amazed at how much of the white man's stone was available to them. The steel that had been used on the roofs would have seemed like riches to her father. Sometimes, she wondered where her family was, but she knew that her father, Omeo, didn't wonder about her. She thought often of her mother. Inala would have loved to hold and spoil Ainia, and Alinta pondered what kind of woman her brother, Miro, would someday find. She often watched the aboriginal people who lived along the creek and were making a village for themselves. The conical huts, called wurlies, went up, and they were well built, despite Mel's worries. Alinta knew her husband intended to build them houses, not as luxurious as the stockmen's houses, simpler and just as nice. She was astonished at this house they now lived in. It was huge and still unfinished. She didn't understand it yet, but Mel promised to eventually explain anything she wanted to know. The wonders of the glass windows and the pump that provided fresh water in their kitchen sink still amazed her. She was used to fetching water when she needed it, and she realized the urn she had made so long ago would have been useless in this white man's world. She knew she wanted to be in Mel's world, and her *husband,* her mate seemed to need to have these things around her/him. Alinta was learning so much, and there was still so much she didn't understand, so she stayed quiet and observed. She saw some of the married stockmen and women

embracing their mates, even doing that mouth on mouth kissing that she had so enjoyed with Mel. She wanted more of that herself and wasn't sure how to broach the subject with Mel. She wasn't one to initiate conversation or contact with Mel, so she would wait and see what more there might be between them when Mel said it was time. She trusted the big woman with the manliness inside her.

Mel wasn't sure how to approach her wife. She had told Alinta they would come to know each other more intimately when they were in their own home, but she was nervous about it. She wanted Alinta and had wanted her for so long. They were married, and until now, they hadn't gone beyond kissing, cuddling, and petting. She wanted to know that firm body she had seen so many times as they walked about together, hand in hand. She wanted that body she had felt against herself when they embraced, kissed, or cuddled. Just the thought of it aroused her again, and she hoped that her wife wanted her too. It had been a long time since they married and since they had started to build their home. She knew it was time, and she wanted to make love to her attractive, sexy wife.

There was always so much work to do, and Mel was tired. She knew the work would be never-ending, but she was young, and her body was able to adjust to it. She spent her evenings peacefully and quietly with Alinta and their daughter, and she enjoyed their time together, but there was so much more Mel wanted once Ainia was fed and asleep. She'd hesitated for so long, but things changed one night when she impulsively kissed Alinta before sleeping, a practice she had used to get Alinta used to her touch. Alinta didn't ever discourage her, and Mel wondered what her wife would she do if she took it further.

Mel deepened the kiss, exploring the woman's mouth with her lips and tongue while scenting her fresh and natural odors with her senses.

Alinta had always enjoyed the mouth on mouth kiss that Mel gave her since she had come to understand it was a sign of affection. As Mel used her tongue and encouraged Alinta to use hers, she began to explore Mel's mouth, tasting the flavor of her. She didn't understand as both their breathing increased, but the petting that Mel bestowed on her body always felt good, and she copied it, exploring the big woman's body.

Mel loved the feel of the hesitant then bolder touch of Alinta's strong and supple fingers on her body. Slowly, they began to remove each other's clothing.

The wraps got in the way after a while, but they quickly removed them, and Alinta rubbed around the sides where the wraps seemed to cause redness on the white woman's body. Mel seemed to enjoy it too, and Alinta wanted to please her.

Mel could feel the play on the muscles that she had admired for so long. The petting they had engaged in, while frustrating at times, had revealed only so much, and she hadn't wanted to frighten the other woman with her lust. Tonight, seemed different though. As they both got naked, the feel of each other's bodies was richer and more intense. She knew this was going to be their night and their time.

Naked bodies were something Alinta had seen her entire life but seeing the muscular and much bigger Mel naked for the first time was overwhelming to her senses. She'd glimpsed things in the time they had been together, of course, but she had learned at an early age to avert her eyes and not to stare. Now, in the flickering firelight of the

stove, she was enjoying the light playing on the white woman's large body. She wanted that body against her. She wanted to feel that body holding her down and making her feel things...almost as though she were helpless. Her breathing continued to increase as they kissed and touched, and it puzzled her. Remembering her parents' couplings, she wondered if this feeling was why they did it. She wondered if she would end up with that same vacant look her mother had or if she would feel the intense emotion that seemed to affect her father. She squashed thoughts of her parents and concentrated on Mel.

Mel had seen Alinta in various stages of dress many times, mostly undress as the aboriginal woman had no qualms about going about naked, but this was different. This time, they were both washed up from their day, and the feel in the air as they kissed was different. Mel slowly removed her lips from Alinta's, kissing along her jaw to under her ear, listening to the increased breathing she heard coming from her wife. She felt the smooth and rippling muscles under her fingertips and palms as she caressed the body she so lusted after.

Alinta loved the contrast of her fingers against Mel. Her skin looked so dark against the white skin that had never seen a ray of sunlight under her clothes. It fascinated her, but she also loved the affect it was having on the American woman. She touched everywhere she could reach, copying what Mel was doing to her body and enjoying the sensations she was receiving. She had never thought that a caress could make her feel so good, but it wasn't just any caress or touch, it was Mel's.

Slowly, the two women explored, going much further than they had in past months as they got to know each other. As Mel gently played

around the breasts that fed their daughter, she saw that milk was forming, and she avoided the tips she so badly wanted to lick and suckle, not wanting to deny their daughter the nourishment. She hoped that someday, when Alinta finished breastfeeding and the breasts dried up, she would teach her wife the enjoyment that could be attained by her lover licking and sucking on her breasts. Instead, for now, she continued across the taut belly, noting the few marks from her pregnancy and then lower to the small bush of hair, tickling the hairs and watching her wife's reaction to her touch. She encouraged Alinta to spread her legs, her own leg coming between them to rub gently at the Y.

Alinta had touched herself there occasionally but had never thought she'd enjoy being touched there by another human being. Mel seemed to find pleasure in the moisture that came from her body. Much to her surprise, the feel of the bigger woman's thigh between her legs made her grind against it slightly, feeling the primitive need of it building as they continued.

Mel smiled against the belly she was kissing, her fingers entwining in the hairs and the folds that had become so odorous and moist beneath her. She explored and heard the intake of Alinta's breath as her fingers touched the nerve endings and rubbed. Slowly, she rubbed up and down the slit, noting the moisture increasing, almost sousing the palm of her hand. Mel knew Alinta wasn't yet ready for too many intimacies, even though her own mouth was watering in anticipation of the tastes. The odors she sensed were telling her how good it would be. Mel desperately wanted to taste there but would save that for another

time.   Instead, her fingers continued to explore and give her wife pleasure, one creeping inside to see how the wild woman reacted.

It wasn't at all like that man's invasion of her body, and Alinta enjoyed the feel of Mel inside her.   When one finger became two and they curled slightly, she was in shock at the sensations that pulsed in her body, and she became slightly limp when Mel hit her G spot. Alinta hadn't known these feelings existed inside her, and she couldn't have resisted even if she wanted to as Mel expertly played her body. She certainly didn't want the woman to stop now.   She wanted more, and her own fingers pulled at Mel's shoulders, encouraging her.

Mel began to pump, her thumb plying the nubbin of flesh that had arisen on the outside, her fingers at first stiff and straight, then bending slightly to find the sentient flesh inside.   She could tell Alinta's passions were building by listening to the anguished breathing and feeling the claw-like fingers on her shoulders.   Mel was becoming more and more excited as she realized the passions in her wild wife.   She pumped harder, making sure to hit her G spot and rub the clit that was standing up more prominently than before.

At the time of crisis, the first time she had ever felt this way in her life, Alinta's primitive instincts came to the forefront, and she bit Mel's shoulder, totally unaware that she was doing this.

Mel couldn't believe the passions displayed before her.   She felt the pain of Alinta's teeth as they bruised and broke the skin on her shoulder, but she didn't stop, driving her wife higher and higher.   Her own lips were sucking on skin and making hickies as she continued to pump her and listen to her crises, exciting herself as she made her wife come.   She moved up, brushing the biting teeth from her shoulder as

she covered Alinta's body with her own. She watched her wife come undone with what she suspected was her first ever orgasm. Little cries came from the smaller woman's mouth, building as she reached her crises, and Mel quickly kissed her to capture the roar of completion that unknowingly escaped from the woman. She arched, her legs clasping Mel's hand between them almost painfully. In the aftermath, as the woman writhed beneath her, Mel kept her warm with her own heated and sweaty body, enjoying the little spasms that squeezed her fingers.

"Are you okay?" Mel asked a while later as she pulled a blanket over their naked bodies, glancing at Ainia to make sure they hadn't woken the baby. The little one was still sleeping, her lips moving as though she were sucking as she dreamed.

"Ya, okay," Alinta whispered back, touching her fingers wonderingly as they tingled, and the blood returned. She had never known such a feeling, and it unnerved her. She opened her eyes to look up at Mel, who was looking down at her with love and tenderness as she held her. She looked away bashfully and Mel just held her closer, understanding what she was too shy to say.

CHAPTER SIX

With the surplus of men, some wanting to return to civilization as soon as possible to spend the money Mel had arranged for them to be paid, Mel tried to utilize those whose skills she needed the most. While one crew continued to work inside what would become her home, finishing walls, putting up more walls, and insulating exterior walls, she was busy elsewhere. She knew her building skills were not as strong as her organizational skills, and she had a lot of other responsibilities.

The sheer number of sheep they now owned required more folds to be built quickly, if the sheep weren't going to chew down to the roots of the grasses available to them, and she took crews of men to the various spots she had noted on the track leading southeast. While they were doing this, she sent men to the other folds with some of the new

sheep, swapping out at least half of the Merinos in each fold with some of the new mixed breeds. This way, her breeding program for next year would mix the breeds even further. She had missed that opportunity this year as she had already sent her rams in among the various flocks of Merinos in the folds. Some of the rams she saw in the mixed batches were heartier, healthier in some cases, bigger, and looked meatier. She wanted more wool and thought that a stockier or heavier sheep might be valuable at some point, if she had to sell her sheep for the mutton. She would let those rams in with the sheep next year, although from what Braun had told her, they had already serviced the mixed breeds on the way out. She sighed at this information, having no idea when the lambs from these mixed breeds would be due and warning her stockmen accordingly.

The men returning with the half flocks of Merinos were given an equal amount of the mixed sheep and directed down the track to the new folds that Mel and her men were building.

It always amazed Mel how much quicker things went when she had help on her projects. Having gone it alone the first year, and in some respects, most of her life, it struck her as odd to have people around her who were willing to help her. Although she was paying them, it still made her think about more and more projects she wished to tackle while she had the chance and the men to help. As the rains came down, making it nearly impossible to work on the folds they were building, she came to realize that where there was a will, there was a way. They might not get a lot of the folds built as quickly as they would have in good weather, but they weren't letting the rain stop them completely.

A rider came rushing down the track looking to find Mel at the second of the folds they had built in the rain. The rushing creek had wiped out one corner of the fold, and the stockman, alarmed, had sent word to her where she was working on the fourth fold. They had come back to repair it.

"Mr. Lawrence, there's flooding in the paddock," he gasped, out of breath from the hard ride through the driving rain.

"Which paddock?" she asked, knowing she would soon have to give the paddocks names or numbers to identify them. Having just finished the repairs on this fold, Mel and her men mounted their horses and rushed to follow the man, so they could help the stockman whose sheep were drowning from the onslaught.

Near to tears at the loss of the animals, Mel sent men to check on the other paddocks and folds, and she ordered them to send for help if they needed it, reminding the stockmen to go to high ground with the sheep. The rain tapered off for a day or two, and she and the other men roped the drowned animals they could find, skinned them, and if the meat was still good, they hung it in bags for the men to eat. They burned the entrails, so the scavengers, especially dingoes, wouldn't be attracted by them.

Mel wearily headed back to the home paddock, forgetting that it was on high ground and all animals, including the wild ones, would head to high ground. She was nearly bitten by a snake as she got off her horse. Only the gelding shying at the dangerous visitor kept her from being struck in a vital spot. The snake struck the high leather of her boot. She calmly pulled her gun and shot at its huge body, making her horse start to buck. Turning, she tried to calm the beast, relieved that the snake hadn't struck a vital spot on her or the horse. Finally, she calmed it, but by then her shot had drawn others, and they all looked at the snake, which was still writhing, its body in death throes. One of the men had a machete, and Mel took it from him to slice off the snake's head, pleased when it finally stopped moving. It was a Common Death Adder, although Mel found nothing common about the ugly thing, and she was glad it was dead. One of the aboriginal men came up and asked if he could take it. She knew he meant to use it for food and for the skin, and she gladly gave permission.

"I want the buildings checked and any new tenants evicted," she gestured towards the snake, "and make sure everyone is *extra* careful," she ordered her new head stockman, a man by the name of Peter Winston. He'd shown a natural leadership of the men even before the extra men Braun had brought showed up. "Check the lofts too," she said, looking up into the barn and nearly shuddering.

The man nodded, giving her a salute with a grin to show he understood her distaste for the snakes. Several men immediately began going through the barns, sheds, and other buildings as well as around the paddocks and corrals. Many snakes and even scorpions were dislodged from their hidey-holes, the men poking and prodding with long sticks to keep from being bitten or stung.

"You okay?" Alinta walked up, holding the baby and looking concerned.

"Have I ever mentioned I *hate* snakes?" Mel grinned wryly, looking down at her pant leg where the snake had struck and seeing a hole in her trousers.

Alinta, responding to the joking note in Mel's voice, was smiling, but she lost her smile when she saw the tear in the pants' leg. "He bite you?" she asked, suddenly worried and feeling vulnerable.

"No, he got the leather of my boots is all," Mel reassured her and took her and the baby in her arms in a hug.

"What would we do without you?" Alinta murmured against her shirt. Since they had made love several times now, Alinta had learned love on a level she didn't previously know existed. The physical pleasure this woman gave her was nothing like what she had expected. She hadn't been sure when Mel indicated she wanted more from her physically, but now all her fears had been put to rest. She looked forward to what more she would learn from this woman.

Mel pulled back to look down on the smaller woman. "I've made arrangements, and if anything were to happen to me, you and Ainia would be taken care of as my heirs," she informed her. "But I hope that won't be for a long time in the future. We have a lot to build here, and I'm looking forward to a long life with you."

Alinta smiled, not understanding what Mel meant by *taking care of her and Ainia* or what an *heir* was, but she was pleased that Mel wanted a long life with her. She'd never had a friend, and Mel assured her that she thought of her as her best friend, her mate, and her love. She liked the love part now that she understood it better.

Mel could hear O'Grady, his men, and the others that were helping on the main house. Once the rooms were all finished, there was going to be a lot she had to order from Sydney. Braun had already declined a second trip to the Outback, saying he'd take commissions closer to the coast. This long trip into the Outback had frightened him on some levels, and he knew some of his men felt the same. He could, however, recommend other carters or drayage companies, who would be glad for the work and wouldn't cheat Mel. He was still confused about his mistake of thinking Mel Lawrence was a woman instead of a man. He had gone over his conversations with the solicitor, Saunders, many times in his head.

Eventually, Mel had to reluctantly let the excess men go. Braun and even O'Grady and his men decided it was time to leave, and it would be safer for them to travel together. Despite the rainy season and how miserable they would be on the tracks, they wanted to get back to civilization. O'Grady had been gone over a year with the work on Twin Station and now on Lawrence Station. He'd appreciated the work, the paper that Mel had written out attesting to the excellent work he and his men had done for her, and most of all the healthy draft on the bank in Sydney for him to draw from and pay his men. He was also secretly glad they were leaving since Mel had been so parsimonious in doling out the rum after a day's hard work, sometimes waiting a full week. A man needed a drink more often than that, and he had done good work for her. You would think the man was a preacher the way he spoke of the dangers of the drink.

Mel gave them several carts to use since she had an abundance now with all the supplies that had been hauled in to build her barns and house. They now had a stockroom manned by a man, who asked for the position of storekeeper. Charley Oscar said he had worked on several stations on the Emu Plains, but an accident with a wild boar had cut his career short since few wanted a gimpy stockman. Mel didn't care that he sat most of the day, so long as he kept an account of all the supplies. She gave him the job, and he used a crutch to hobble around and do his duties. He not only kept good accounts but maintained the building in a neat and orderly manner. Many was the time they had to send someone out to the various paddocks and their folds to resupply the men, and she didn't want waste. She drew on their supplies, giving them to the men heading back to Wilcannia and eventually, Sydney.

"I thank you for the opportunity," Braun told her, shaking her hand before he mounted up. The bullocks pulling the carts carried a few men but most were mounted on their own horses. Mel had given him a packet of letters to mail for her and a couple to hand deliver to Saunders when he saw him in Sydney.

One of the men had knocked together a kitchen table and chairs for Mel, and she used lantern light when she sat at it nightly, writing letters and teaching Alinta to read and write. She smiled at her wife's progress, surprised and pleased at how eager and willing she was to learn these things. She was also quick, and Mel had to think hard to keep ahead of her. Alinta had taken over some of the home paddock chores, which freed Mel to work farther afield. Mel wasn't always home, but Alinta welcomed her back with open arms each time she rode in.

"I would like to ride with you sometime," Alinta mentioned, finding caring for the chickens, the ducks, and the garden in between rain squalls to be boring. Ainia was a handful but calmed when she rode with them. It was becoming harder as Mel was going farther afield to get the folds done, despite the rain. She wanted to get the men on the other folds north of their location but knew that would have to wait. One of the letters she had sent out was looking for someone to start

building fencing for her. She simply didn't have enough men, and she wanted to start enclosing her paddocks, so they didn't lose stock if they got out of the folds.

"You want to go out to the folds with me?"

Alinta nodded, watching her husband carefully. She didn't want to sit in the big, empty house that was now essentially done except for the furniture that would have to wait until more carts came all the way from Sydney. They were living in the kitchen, which was nice and warm, but Alinta preferred to be outdoors, and few of the stockmen's wives associated with her since she was the owner's wife. She knew still others didn't like her because she was an Aborigine. What she didn't know was her husband was aware of their disdain, and if anything came of it, she was ready to deal with it. So far, their husbands had proven to be good workers, or she would have already sent them on their way back to Sydney with Braun and his other men.

Mel was trying to be fair to her wife. She couldn't have sat at the house either, but she had real ideas of the role of wife, and her wife fit none of them. She was a wild thing, used to being out of doors and very independent. She couldn't put Alinta in a mold. Mel smiled, showing she was going to give her wife favorable news. "Sure. Anytime you want to go, you just saddle up and get Ainia ready," she promised. One of the other letters she had sent was an ad for people who knew they could work in the Outback, not only stockmen but help in the house. Although Alinta was a lot cleaner than she had been, she wouldn't keep the house the way Mel wanted. She didn't allow the dirt to build up on her person anymore either, bathing regularly since Mel had shown her how much she liked it. Mel had lived long enough in

the dirt and hadn't really minded it, but now, she wanted her home to be a sanctuary, and there was no way that a primitive woman growing up on the Outback of Australia could understand the white man's ways or the levels of maintenance that Mel would expect. She needed to be shown how to create and maintain the house Mel wanted here. Barring a trip to Sydney, which Mel knew would cause her wife endless anxiety, the only way to show her was by having someone come to them and teach her.

Remembering the houses they had encountered on the trek from Sydney as well as the original house on Twin Station, Mel knew that she didn't want anything basic. She knew a lot of stations didn't care what they lived in as long as they had their sheep. The animals were far more important to them than what they lived in. This ranch, or rather, this station she was building out here on the Outback was to be a sanctuary for them and their families. Already, many made the trek to enjoy the sight of the hidden valley, walking between the creek in front of the big house where the stockmen's houses and Aborigines' village were located, up past the barns and corrals to the almost hidden track, and down into the large valley behind the house. Mel had been right. The view from the master bedroom overlooking the valley was incredible, and sunrise was her favorite time. If it wasn't so cold that they were forced to huddle in the kitchen, she would have insisted they sleep on the floor in the master bedroom while they waited for the furniture and beds to come from Sydney. She'd asked Mr. Saunders to get input from his wife and Mrs. Waters, the seamstress, before purchasing furniture for her home. She had described just what she was looking, so they could send everything with their supplies. The curtains and the draperies could be sewn here on the station when the sewing machine and materials she had asked Mrs. Waters to obtain were sent. She expected the supplies to come with the carters she had contracted with, knowing the shearers would come from Twin Station when they finished the sheep there. Meanwhile, Mel had to keep all the sheep alive through the terrible winter rains they were experiencing.

One stormy day, Mel had planned to take a crew out to the final fold they were building—the first thing people would find when they came up the track from Wilcannia—but they found the rain was coming down so hard that only indoor work could be done. As they were still building tables and stalls in the various barns and sheds, they decided to concentrate on that. Mel was soaked from merely running from the house to the big barn, and she was grateful for the sheepskin coat she had made so long ago. It was cold, the winds howled, and she closed the door on the barn with a bang as she entered. The cows that were indoors looked up from where they were chewing their cuds. The few milk cows they now owned stayed indoors during this inclement weather, and their manure was being shoveled into a cart kept there for just that purpose. This manure would be hauled down to the compost piles around the gardens when it was full. Mel had expanded the gardens considerably with all the extra people on the station. Fresh vegetables were a nice treat to the stockmen, who only saw people once a month, if that, as they watched their charges, the sheep.

"Hey, boss," one of the men greeted her as she blinked in the light of the lanterns, her eyes slowly adjusting to the light. The lanterns were hung in a way that kept them away from the animals, so they

couldn't be accidentally knocked over but still provided plenty of light, so the men could see to do the necessary chores.

"Hey," she grunted in return as she shook her head, scattering drops of water. She took off her hat and hung it and her coat on some pegs. The barn was already warm from all the animals inside it. A dog greeted her, and she petted the bitch, noticing her litter in the corner of a stall they had just built. Mel followed the bitch and gazed at the pups, wondering about this latest batch. Already, the previous pups from her other two dogs were half grown and becoming well trained. They followed their dam and the other dogs, watching them and learning even more than they would from the humans, who taught them the hand signals, whistles, and verbal commands.

A crash of lightning flared outside before the thunder sounded, and the rain lashed against the windows in the lofts where they shone down onto the pathways of the large barn. She looked up, hoping the expensive windows they had carted all the way out here wouldn't break. She hated that even a few had broken this way. Some openings were boarded over for now until new panes could be brought out from the city. The few extra panels they had stored had already been used, and the extra panels for the house didn't fit these openings.

"They're buildin' over in the second barn," one of the men grunted while milking a cow before turning his attention back to his chore.

"Thank you," Mel said as she walked through the pathway down the center of the barn. Most of the interior was unfinished, and she kind of liked the openness of the huge, cavernous building, but slowly, it was getting finished off. Someone had already put in the long row of stanchions for the cows that even now were being milked. One of the stockmen's wives knew how to make cheese and was busy working with their excess milk.

Mel entered the second barn, this one in the Monitor Style, which complemented the Gambrel style of the big barn, now called the First Barn. Its dormers and gables gave the barn a regal sense, and Mel loved that it matched the Big House. She could hear the rain beating down on the metal roofs, a fine protection against the elements. There were wood and tar sheets underneath that metal as extra security against Mother Nature, but nothing could match the security of those large, corrugated, metal sheets. Mel imagined her accountant had probably had a coronary at the expense of everything she had ordered, but her bank account could afford it, and she'd decided long ago to have the best and make it long-lasting.

Mel helped set up the platforms they would use when the shearers came, placing them in the shearing shed, which was eerily quiet with only a few of the men working. The wide floors would be busy come spring when they sheared all the sheep Mel now owned. Right now, winter was here in earnest, and they had to get things ready. The day passed quickly, and Mel had to be reminded to eat when the men headed for the barracks with its now adjacent hall and full-time cook. He was a mate of Charley Oscar's, who also rode the long distance from Sydney hoping for a job and prepared to ride the long distance back if he was disappointed. When Mel had asked him if he could cook, and surprisingly, he could, she had made him the cook, so the men didn't have to take turns doing that chore. They'd built the hall and put in tables with long benches, so the men could eat and socialize. Behind the hall was a wash house with a bathtub, showers, and sinks, so the men could bathe if they desired. Few did, but they could shave in comfort over the sinks, and the bath house had running water with hot water from the reservoir behind the stove.

Mel laughed at herself. Everything in Australia, not just the Darling/Cobdogla River, was upside down. She was still having a hard time getting used to the seasons. Winter officially began on the first of June and spring began on the first of September. It was hard to imagine Christmas in the middle of what she considered summer months, but that's the way it was down here.

The amount of rain that fell astonished her. It explained why she had seen debris high in some of the trees and bushes many times as she was wandering about looking for good places to put folds and paddocks. These places flooded out for good reason. She was glad she had put her home station on the side of a hill, the rest of the hill blocking one side of it from the worst of the winds. Even the lush valley it overlooked was inundated with water, and the dams they had erected were far under water if not washed away by the torrential rains that showed no signs of letting up.

"Have to make up when it dry all summer," Alinta philosophized, and Mel grinned. Her wife was a very wise woman; however, that did give her food for thought. As she planned out the folds to the north, which she would build when the rain let up enough that they could go out, she looked for creeks or billabongs that had springs or would remain wet year-round. It would be foolish to build a fold, only to watch her sheep die for lack of water. Having less sheep in some of these areas would mean less work for the stockmen, who worked these drier areas. She still planned for smaller flocks since she remembered how terrifying it was to have such a large flock that the animals didn't fit into the permanent fold, and they also had the worry of dingoes going after the lambs.

The winter passed and they kept busy with all the indoor work, getting things ready for the spring rush, but there was enough outdoor work to keep them equally busy. All the sheep were out in folds with very few being kept at the home paddocks except those for consumption. The sheep were due to start lambing and remembering how Foster had brought at least one flock into the home pasture to help the stockmen, Mel decided to do that too. She also planned to send out extra men to help the lonely stockmen in the far folds, knowing she would never again have enough stockmen to do this in the future as her flocks grew. She emphasized that the sheep came first, and if the stockmen went without sleep, that was part of their jobs. She knew what the season was about to throw at them, but she hadn't anticipated the flock coming from Sydney being randomly bred and most of them arriving pregnant from the rams being mixed in with the ewes. She was just preparing to send out stockmen from the home ranch when one of the men, who was supplying the various stockmen, raced back to tell her that the lambs were already coming.

The flock that was brought into the home paddock held off longer than Mel anticipated, and she went out into the paddocks to help the other stockmen, well remembering the nightmare she had endured last

year with the unending birthing going on around her in the large flock. Even with help, they were constantly at it, and she could only hope the men in the various folds and paddocks were as conscientious as she. She had heard from grazer's talk that something like thirty-three percent of lambs could be lost to dingoes and other predators if a stockman wasn't diligent.

While letting the sheep out of the folds to graze, many birthed along the way. Sheep would graze for up to seven hours a day, usually in the early morning but sometimes in late afternoon before sunset. They had to get them out there while they were simultaneously giving birth. Because of the discrepancy of the breeding of the two flocks, the birthing went on for weeks and weeks. Just when they thought they were done, some more would give birth, and then, the sheep that Mel had bred, the Merinos, started giving birth. It was a nightmare, and all the men were blurry-eyed and resentful of the intense work that lasted far too long.

Dingoes were bad in various spots, and many times, the stockmen couldn't cope. They lost not only lambs but sheep and dogs. Dingoes would rip open the throat of the animal they were after and continue the hunt without stopping to eat right away. They were worse in the early morning hours while teaching their young to hunt, but they could attack at any time. Seeing the sheep's throats ripped out angered and saddened Mel in equal measures, and she killed all dingoes on sight, preferring to shoot them between the eyes if she happened to see them in the brush around the folds. She gave a bonus to one stockman when she found a dozen dingoes that had been strung up by their tails and were hanging from the trees. This news spread and other stockmen imitated his behavior, bragging that they too would get a dozen, but Mel only gave the bonus if they had a dozen or more. The carnage when dingoes got in amongst her sheep was horrible, and they were in the business of raising sheep.

Mulesing and docking the sheep was up to the individual stockmen. The different breeds made it more difficult in some cases, but Mel and the others she sent out to help pitched in where they could. Alinta even helped this year. Sometimes, Ainia was strapped to her back and other times, she was toddling about. They kept an eye on the little girl, so a dingo wouldn't get her, knowing the dingo wouldn't have discriminated between the young of a sheep or a human. Mel made sure she was always nearby to protect their daughter when Ainia was on the ground.

CHAPTER SEVEN

Next on their schedule after the mad rush of the extended birthing season was the work involved in shearing. The shearers arrived from Twin Station bearing letters from Carmen and Fabiola. They marveled at the new buildings that were enormous, clean, and brightly lit, and they immediately set to work. Mel sent for the various flocks, knowing most of her men would instinctively know it was time to come in for the yearly shear by the time of year, and the others would have seen the shearers as they passed by the various folds.

The sheep looked uncomfortable, and Mel wanted their long fleeces removed before summer hit. The mulesing had almost healed on the lambs, and if the flock came along slow, the lambs thrived, but again, dingoes and other predators were a problem. There was no way to solve that problem, and they could only be vigilant.

"Maybe we should come twice a year?" one of the shearers joked, seeing the length of the fleece on some of the sheep.

Mel had heard of some places shearing twice a year but couldn't imagine having this commotion more than once a year. Sheep grew wool continuously and became stressed and uncomfortable with the heat. The wool could become matted and difficult to remove if left uncut. In fact, sheep that escaped the folds and weren't killed by dingoes were called woolies. These animals became feral. Mel had never seen one, but she had heard of them. She wondered how they coped with the length of their wool and if perhaps, at a certain length, the wool slowed its growth.

"Some station near Cobar is trying to raise them sheep that have hair instead of wool," one of the shearers mentioned, never stopping his chatter as he worked the shears effortlessly.

"Hair? Not wool? How do you shear them?" another asked, his unlit pipe in the corner of his mouth because Mel wouldn't allow smoking anywhere near the barns or sheds, insisting it be kept to the barracks and hall.

"You don't," said the first shearer. "They shed like dogs and cats."

The others guffawed, sure he was funning them, but Mel had heard of these sheep and wondered about them. "What happens if you breed 'em to wool-bearing sheep?"

The man eyed the Yank station owner for a second. "I bet you'd have to shear them," he answered. "I hain't seen 'em though, only heard about 'em."

That kind of talk was how rumors were spread, and all the men took it with a grain of salt thinking it was a tall tale, like the stories of bunyips and other bush tales.

"I bet them hair sheep ain't any good for spinnin'," another shearer put in.

"Bet I can shear the most sheep today," another challenged in order to get more work out of his men. All of them took on the challenge.

Mel smiled. A good shearer could shear a sheep in less than two minutes and could remove the entire fleece in one piece. Stompers, men who collected the fleeces, put them in the large bags, and stomped on them to pack the bags full, were kept busy.

"I heard one man sheared eight hundred sheep in nine hours," one commented.

"Bullshit!" several voices rang out in protest. The most a shearer using hand blades could hope for was fifty sheep a day. Although, if their back didn't give out and they didn't stop for a break or food, at one sheep every two minutes or so, they could do lots more than the average of fifty sheep in a day.

Mel grinned at their good-natured ribbing and slightly competitive natures. She'd shorn a few sheep herself but realized she was outclassed by these quickly efficient men. She wouldn't compete with them, and there was no reason to. They did a good job, although occasionally, a newer man would nick one of her sheep and get a ration of shit from his buddies over it. She liked that they seemed determined not to cut her sheep, who looked so helpless as they were stripped of their winter jackets.

"Get some of that mixture my wife made up onto that lot there," Mel called, seeing how some of the breeds seemed more likely to burn in the hot sun. The scabs that formed from the sunburn disgusted her, but Alinta knew of plants and mixtures she could make that healed such burns, and she had made plenty once she realized Mel didn't want the scabs on her sheep. It looked painful, and the poor sheep were treated badly by most men. Mel didn't want to add to their misery. She knew the men thought nothing of the animals, but her heart hurt for all of them, from the abandoned lambs whose mothers wouldn't feed them to these poor sunburned sheep. Looking at the Leicester, who reminded her of small llamas with their ears sticking out, she wondered what their offspring would look like when they were bred with the Merinos. She now regretted mixing the flocks since there was no way to breed the other rams with her Merinos only or put the Merino rams onto the others.

"Can you separate some out?" she asked a couple of the stockmen, including her head stockman, Peter, in the conversation.

"What's that in aid of?" he asked as he complied. She explained her mistake in mixing the sheep too soon, and he understood, even if he thought it a foolish waste of time. Still, Mel was a good employer and paid on time every month, so he wouldn't argue. He tried to help the men sort the now shorn sheep, sending the stockmen back to their folds in the various paddocks short some sheep until several flocks were in at the same time.

Mel watched as the shorn sheep were separated then released back among the baaing and maaing lambs, who were nearly frantic while their mums were kept away. It amazed her how quickly they were

sorted, and the upset was soon forgotten as the sheep easily found their babies. Mel also kept the rams in at the home paddocks, sorting out the different breeds and sending them down into the valley where several folds were set up down its length now that the flood waters were long gone.

The bags of wool were stacked up in the shearing sheds and reached all the way to the roof. Mel considered filling the many carts they had available, but she was expecting her carters any day. They would fill their carts first and would only fill her carts if they ran out of room, but she was certain the carters she had contracted with would anticipate their needs and bring plenty of carts.

The final flocks were in, shorn, sorted, and back on their way as the shearers went on down the road, receiving cash money for their work instead of the bags of wool they were usually paid. They promised to be at Mel's station first next year, as they were eager to earn that money. That meant Lawrence Station would be serviced before Twin Station, and Mel hoped that wouldn't cause hard feelings with her neighbors and friends, Carmen and Fabiola. Mel wondered about Harold, unsure what his story was and why he gave her an odd feeling whenever she saw him.

The shearers passed the long line of carters on the track. They were also bringing supplies and orders that Mel had written and requested from her solicitor. As they shared a fire, they exchanged pleasantries and impressions of the Lawrence Station the shearers had just left.

"Mel Lawrence?" one man asked, squinting. "Big man? Blocky face and brown hair? No beard?"

"Yes, that would be him," the lead shearer replied, reaching for some damper to go with the meal they were sharing.

The man nodded thoughtfully, having thought the last name a coincidence.

The carters saw the signs Mel had staked last year, which were pointing the way to Lawrence Station. They saw that while the track might be relatively new from Wilcannia, it already looked well worn and broken in here. The outback sometimes left signs for years, and other times, Mother Nature wiped out the signs in a season. They passed the first of many folds, taking advantage of the water spots as the thin ribbon of track wound around the hills and stopped at the various creeks and billabongs. The men had speculated at the many supplies—a tremendous amount by anyone's standards—as well as the guards their boss had hired, who rode horses and carried multiple guns to guard their precious train. The drivers that had been hired hadn't witnessed the loading of the many carts, so they had no idea what was in them. Occasionally, they had tried to look but sacks cushioned much of the load and hid what was inside. Tarps held the weather at bay as an occasional rainstorm came through, but as summer came on in earnest and spring tapered off, it was becoming hotter the farther west they traveled.

"Well, we're closer," one man remarked, seeing a sign that read Lawrence Station and the wood pointing the way.

"Ain't that mean we're halfway?" another asked, seeing several men's eyes widen when they didn't realize he was teasing. The hundreds of miles they had already traveled had left some of the drivers in shock. The Outback seemed oppressive to them, as though the

nights were creeping in on them. They huddled close to the fires, burning more wood than necessary and making the light shine farther from their overly large fires. Even the days weren't much better as the distances between stations had increased the farther west they went. Since Wilcannia, they had only seen a couple indications of stations before they saw the sign that clearly read Lawrence Station, to those who could read.

Mel was pleased to see signs of the drays coming down the track. She'd worried for a while now since the shearers had left, and she was hoping they wouldn't be delayed for any reason. The mail she had gotten from her solicitor expressed concern at the large sums of money she was going through in her desire to build up the large station she was establishing. She hoped her replies expressed her absolute joy in finding the hidden valley, how much the Outback meant to her, and her delight in finally finding peace in Australia. She knew if the drover the lawyer hired expressed any confusion over Mel being a man or a woman, at least her signature on the letters would match the documents she had signed in Sydney. She hoped she never had to travel back there to prove her identity, knowing it was over one thousand miles away.

"Men come?" Alinta asked, pointing with her chin down the trail as she played with Ainia on the lawn that Mel kept in front of the house. The rains had provided them with luxuriant growth, and she'd been cutting it back with scythe, finally assigning that chore to one of the stockmen's sons as she gave other children work to do around the home paddock. The children must learn to be useful citizens, and she had talked to Peter Winston as well as Alinta about someday having a school at the station for both the white children and the Aborigines.

Mel said that Ainia could have a tutor, if Alinta wanted, but the aboriginal woman wasn't quite sure what a tutor was. Mel explained, but Alinta hadn't heard of that before and wasn't going to worry about it now since Ainia was still too young.

"Yes, I think it's our supplies for the house," Mel said, squinting. She had also sent away for reading glasses, annoyed that her vision had worsened as she got older and was making it harder to read the letters and brochures she got in the mail.

The men began to unload the carts, and Mel directed the furniture into the house, telling Alinta to show them where each item went in the house. Since the woman didn't know what some of the furniture was, Mel told her in a whisper, so she looked knowledgeable. Charlie Oscar directed the supplies into the stockrooms, marking them against the manifest that had accompanied the drayage company.

"Sir, I believe this is yours," the head carter came up to hand a box to Mel. "I was instructed to make sure I handed it to the station owner."

"Granger?" Mel exclaimed. "George Granger?" she asked, recognizing the man.

"Mel? Mel Lawrence?" he returned, smiling. "I thought the name was familiar, but I wasn't sure."

She shook the man's hand as he set the slatted box down. It smelled a little gamy, and a hissing noise could be heard coming from inside. "Is that my cat?" she asked, worried. "Where's the other one?"

"Yes, she's an ornery cuss and pregnant, as you requested, I understand," he said, sounding put out. "The male escaped, and I think something got him." He sounded sorry but had thought it odd to be transporting felines.

She nodded ruefully over the loss of the tomcat. "Good," she exclaimed, clapping her hands together. "If the snakes don't get her and her kittens, we will have something else to help keep down the mice and rats. I hate those snakes!" she said, shuddering.

He laughed, understanding Mel's fear of snakes; a lot of men hated snakes. "I thought it an odd request, but now, I understand," he said, indicating the cat.

"Let's put her in the shade on the porch, so she's out of the way and downwind," Mel said as she went to pick up the box. "Did you let her out on the trip?"

"Many times, but I almost lost her a couple of times, and she shit in there so often that I couldn't keep up," he admitted. "She's been well fed, but she's a bitch, if you don't mind my sayin'."

Mel laughed, charmed by the idea that the cat was mean. "It's good to see you again, and I hope the trip wasn't too arduous. We have the wool all stacked and ready for your men once the carts are empty. If you need more carts, I have a few I can sell you too," she informed him as they put the cat on the porch and headed back down the steps, standing aside for some men bringing in a bedstead. Alinta smiled happily as she recognized what it was from Mel's descriptions. She knew where one of those went. After all, they had six bedrooms upstairs, and the key word in bedstead was bed.

"Is that the girl you gambled with Bradley for?" George asked before he thought it through, surprised to see her looking so…good.

"Careful there, Granger. That's my wife, Alinta," Mel warned, feeling prickly at hearing the name Bradley, the man who had abused Alinta so badly. She supposed she owed Bradley a debt for fathering Ainia, but she didn't want anyone to know that she wasn't the toddler's natural father. No one needed to know that. She saw the toddler standing there, staring at the commotion, a puppy she had been playing with sitting at her feet. She wondered how the little girl would react to the kittens when they arrived.

"Oh, yes. Of course," he said, backing off immediately. Things that might be said about a slattern would certainly earn him a punch on the nose if they were directed at a wife, and he wasn't even sure it was the same woman. This one looked him in the eye confidently, and the other woman—he didn't remember if she even had a name—had looked down-trodden, dirty, and sickly to him. This one had on proper clothes, her hair was combed, and she was very clean. Now that he really thought about it, the other one had been a mere girl, and this was a *woman*.

"Let's get a move on with those supplies. I'm sure you are anxious to begin your trip back," Mel hinted broadly, distracting him.

George took the hint. Besides, he *was* anxious to get going. He hoped to hit another one or two stations, depending on the amount of wool he collected here and how many carts he had left. He liked hearing that Lawrence had some carts he was willing to part with. He might just take him up on the offer. He glanced at the blonde-haired, blue-eyed, little girl with her finger in her mouth as she watched the men moving about emptying the carts, and then, he saw Lawrence pick her up. She looked so much like the man that he immediately

dismissed any thoughts the woman could be that slave girl from long ago. He didn't think an Aborigine could have birthed a child that looked so white.

"Mr. Lawrence?" Another man approached Mel as she spoke with her daughter and pointed out the animals to her.

"Yes, I'm Lawrence," Mel replied, looking at the man and waiting. She saw Alinta exit the house, glance towards the hissing box on the porch, and frown. Then, seeing Mel holding Ainia, she headed for her. The two men who had taken in the bedstead followed her down the steps.

"I'm Oakley. Yer solicitor, Saunders, said you were looking for someone to build fencin'?" he asked, taking his hat off out of respect to the station owner.

"How many men did you bring with you, Mr. Oakley?"

"I got a dozen with me, and a couple of Granger's might want to stay on. They's said they'd like to, but I think 'e's gonna need 'em to drive all dem carts," he said philosophically. "We been buildin' fences back near Bathurst and gone down to Wagga Wagga and as fur north as Dubbo, but when I hears about that solicitor feller lookin' for a team, I says I should apply, and he recommended I should." The man took a letter out of his dirty shirt and handed it to Mel. Mel handed Ainia off to a smiling Alinta, who went off to look at the other furniture that was being unpacked amongst the other supplies. The wood had been cleverly cushioned by bags of food that were even now being taken into the storeroom.

Mel quickly read the letter. The solicitor had a couple things to say about the expense of fencing on the station as well as the letters of recommendation the man had evidently supplied. She smiled, understanding the man's concern and appreciating it at the same time.

"Took me a while to find them there drayage company comin' out here," he added, evidently thinking that Mel was annoyed at how long it had taken them to arrive.

"Well, it's a far piece," she admitted, finishing the letter and folding it again. "I hope your men can handle the remoteness of the area. I want to start on my southern border and go from there. I hope to enclose quite a few paddocks, so my men won't lose any sheep."

"Are you goin' to use split rail or–?"

Mel spotted the nice mahogany bedroom set she had ordered and smiled at the man carrying it. "That goes in the master bedroom," she told him, interrupting George as Alinta hurried to show him where it went. The last one had gone in a spare bedroom as Alinta only knew that it went in a bedroom. She knew what master bedroom meant.

Mel turned back to the man waiting patiently before her. "I'll ride out with you and your men and show you my southernmost line where I want the fencing to go. We'll use a combination of split rail and relocate brush, if needed. Depends on the location and what's available," she advised, and the man nodded. He had many shovels, axes, and other tools that would be necessary to build the fences. Mel would be providing them with food supplies and of course, paying them for their time. They discussed what she expected before Mel suggested the men take a day or two to become acquainted with the home paddock while she got things squared away with the drayage company and the carters.

That night, the village set up a terrible ruckus with their digeridoos. The men, celebrating the arrival of the supplies and the men who had made the long trip, enjoyed the rum that Mel sent down. Having been just re-supplied, she put the large order of new rum down in her cellar, so no one could overindulge. Only a limited supply was kept in the stockroom, and Charley would give that out to the stockmen he resupplied. Everyone had a good time, and Mel and Alinta walked down to make an appearance at the stockmen's fire, in the hall, and down by the creek in the village. Ainia was perched on Alinta's hip as they walked. Mel compared Ainia to the aboriginal children there and found she looked whiter than the Aborigines, her father's genes being prevalent, but sometimes, in the right light, Alinta also looked white in profile. Even Alinta's hair wasn't as tight and springy as these peoples. Ainia's hair was blonde, but aboriginal children were usually blonde until they got older and their hair color changed. They had no idea yet if Ainia's hair would remain blonde.

The head man, Djalu, approached Mel as he saw her family watching the dancing and music.

"Good evening, Djalu," Mel said respectfully, knowing she had the name right since Alinta had helped her work on her pronunciation.

"Misster Lawwrrence," the man said deferentially, trying to pronounce the American name, and it was apparent he had put as much practice into saying her name as she had put into pronouncing his name correctly.

"Any of your men want some work? We are going out in two days to build fences," she told him. The men had helped around the home paddock, and a few of the boys were becoming jackaroos or apprentice

stockmen, but both Peter Winston and Alinta had doubts about whether they could be taught. Mel was still hopeful that if they were taught young, they could grow up and learn to be good stockmen.

The man nodded to show he understood. Mel would pay them in supplies, and he had a fondness for the sweets the white man sometimes kept in their supplies. The children almost had to fight the old man for their fair share when Mel doled them out. He said he would tell the men, and those who wanted to work would join them. He looked curiously at Ainia, wondering at the child of mixed races.

Mel and Alinta headed back to the main house. The mosquitos down by the creek were ferocious. "If only we could get rid of the flies and mosquitos," Mel complained as she increased her stride to get up the hill and away from the water where the mosquitos bred. Still, they followed her in the tall grasses, and the flies plagued them during the day.

"I make mix," Alinta told her, referring to the plants she ground together that seemed to repel the bugs that the white men were so plagued with. They didn't bother her nearly as much except after she bathed.

"I'd appreciate it," Mel said, slapping at another of the bugs that was biting her arm. She knew she'd have welts all over but for now, there was nothing they could do but suffer them.

They passed by the celebration going on inside and outside the hall, and Mel motioned to Peter. "Make sure they shut things down and put the fires out by midnight. We have a full day tomorrow."

"You got it, boss," he said with a cheeky grin, giving a salute with his hat towards the missus. He'd had a bit of rum himself, but they all deserved to let off a bit of steam now and then, and Mel didn't really mind. So long as the men did their work, these little indulgences of theirs were fine. She only got angry when men like Shamus O'Grady wanted to get rip-roaring drunk every other night and slow down the pace of the work. Any man who couldn't hold their liquor was restricted or eventually let go. Already, one had moved on with the shearers. He was angry for being discharged, but he had known the rules and his work had suffered.

CHAPTER EIGHT

Mel took the crew, including several aboriginal men, her wife, and her daughter, and headed down the track towards Twin Station, although she would have liked to stay at the house instead to place all the new furniture where she wanted it. Along with the beds, dressers, tables, and other furniture she ordered, linens, bedclothes, mattresses, curtains, and other things she wanted to put up had also arrived. She sighed. There was so much to do, and she knew it might take years, but she wanted her home to be finished and as comfortable as possible.

She'd left men with instructions on the supplies. Several were taking horses and supplies out to the men in the folds, and one was replacing the glass windows that had been broken. She'd washed the cat and made it a box in the house, instructing the new maid to take care of it for her. They'd made up a bedroom in the basement for the

new maid, who had been grateful for the private space. She had a real bed, and the room even had its own window. She felt cozy in the dry basement and promised to not only look after the cat but to start cleaning the house from top to bottom. Mel had wanted to be there, but she could always move things later.

Alinta certainly didn't understand or care, but she knew it was important to Mel. While she could have helped the maid, she didn't really know what to do with these odd things that didn't make much sense to her. She did appreciate the warm house and the beautiful windows that showed their Outback to her, but she preferred being out of doors. She loved that she was riding a horse with Ainia on the saddle before her and seeing more of her beloved Outback. She was developing a sense of ownership for the land that she had never felt before. She laughed when she thought about Mel *taming* the land. No one owned the land or tamed it; the land owned *you*, and *you* conformed to the land. Even the great house on the hill might someday be taken away by the winds that came with the winter rains.

As Mel rode along and watched for anything that might spook the horses, she was also lost in thought dreaming about what she wanted for her station. She laughed at the antics of the wild birds, cockatoos, and others she didn't even know the names of. Her men had learned that the Yank was interested in the names of all the animals and birds that were native to Australia, and she had learned a lot about them, but there was nothing like seeing them roaming free on the plains or in the bush and having them pointed out to her. Red kangaroos and wallabies bounded about the hills. Her wife could see things none of the men could see; her eyesight and powers of observance were amazing. Mel

smiled at her frequently during their ride, even though much of it was spent in silence, the people rarely talking as they rode along. The birds made enough noise for a platoon of men and horses. The cries of parrots, the insane laughter of a bird called a kookaburra, which Mel thought was made up until another person confirmed the odd name, and the calls of other birds made for a constant background of noise. She didn't mind. She loved the relative silence because the Outback was never completely silent, and she could hear the wildlife around them as they rode.

They camped near the second fold that first night, which was the third fold Mel had built with her own hands so long ago. Chatting with the stockman, her attention was drawn to an odd formation of rocks that Alinta pointed out, which contained ancient drawings. Mel could feel something in the air when she visited the rocks. At first, she thought perhaps, it was the torches they were carrying to look at the drawings, but she instinctively knew it was more than that. She glanced at Alinta and saw she felt it too. Even Ainia moved uneasily, sensing something. They didn't stay long, but the feeling persisted long after they had left the site.

"Want me to blast it?" the stockman offered.

"Does it interfere with the sheep eating grass around there?" Mel countered, lifting an eyebrow.

"No, but I thought you might want it...gone?" he hesitated, unsure what the owner meant. The rock formation gave him the willies.

"No, leave it. The Aborigines who roamed this land forever might consider it sacred. I have no problem with it remaining. They are welcome to it. It is theirs for all time. Leave it alone," she instructed

him, looking at him intensely to convey how important it was to her. Blast it, indeed! "I'd rather you hunted dingoes than worry about some drawings that some long gone people put on some rocks."

"I've been hunting!" he protested immediately.

"Yes, but there are always more. There seems to be an unending number of dingoes," she sighed. It was true. Even when she or others had wiped out a colony, other animals eventually moved in. "I know. All you can do is try," she consoled him, but the distraction from the cave drawings had worked, and they began to talk about the sheep and the fencing operations she and the other men were there for. "We could remove some of that brush," she indicated some foliage around the fold. "It'll give fewer hiding places for dingoes and other scavengers. We want grass, not brush," she advised her stockmen, and they nodded. Cutting back some of the brush would give them something to do during the day as the sheep grazed, and it would create areas where more grass could grow.

Mel started at what she considered her southernmost and western corner, choosing a spot that didn't infringe on Twin Station to the south and the desert-like area to the west. She was down off the strange hills she had noted when she had come here with Carmen and Fabiola so long ago. Their domed tops were very distinctive. She had thought to start the fencing on the actual hills but thought it too strenuous, not only for the fence builders but also the animals that would graze here. She stayed a week to help the men put up the fence along the southern border and help to construct a gate system that didn't impede anyone from the other station. They just needed to lower the fence bars or put them aside to continue the track that led between the two stations.

Using a combination of brush, trees, and deadfalls, they started the fence line. Mel indicated where she wanted them to head north and enclose that first paddock. She then continued north to that first paddock's northeastern border, put up markers and headed west again putting up additional markers along the way until she was at what she considered her western border. It was much more arid in this area.

The trip reminded her of that first year when it was just her and Alinta, the sheep, and the dogs. Once they left the fence builders behind, the three of them were alone, and she was fine with that. She spent her time enjoying her little family and the Outback. She could see Alinta was supremely happy as they sat together at night, the fire crackling merrily but not large enough to impede their view of the night sky. It was endless, beautiful, and theirs as they murmured quietly, so they didn't interrupt the feel of the night upon them as they lay there. Watching Ainia toddle about importantly, picking up sticks and stones and beginning to use nonsense words, was a delight both parents enjoyed. Eventually, they had to go back, but this little trip invigorated them. Slowly, they headed back, marking the western desert-like border in places until they were about even with the home paddock by Mel's estimates. She wasn't sure if the creek that petered out in the desert here was the same creek that ran through the home paddock, and they followed it quite a ways until a cliff impeded their ability to continue. They couldn't go around the cliff, and Mel didn't want to climb it with Ainia along, so they backtracked until they found the track and headed for home.

Mel was thrilled to find the bedrooms put together and found she only had to move a few things. The new maid, Betty Firth, was a godsend, and she smiled shyly at Mel's praise.

Alinta looked around at the furnishings. She didn't understand many of them, but she saw that Mel was pleased, and this pleased her.

The cat had made itself at home, and it was happier now that it was out of the cage and no longer traveling. Its kittens had been born while they were gone, and the mother cat seemed content in the kitchen by the stove and curled up in a box. Betty confided she had burned the crate due to its stench, and Mel agreed with her actions.

Alinta had never seen a cat and had nothing to compare it to. At least the dogs were dingo-like. This cat was in the realm of the horses, cows, and sheep, which her people had never seen. In fact, they weren't native to Australia at all. Only the pigs were creatures that the primitive people would recognize since wild boars were a menace to one and all with their mercurial tempers. She approached the cat with caution and was surprised how soft the fur felt on its offspring. She could see nothing dangerous about these young but examined their feet with the small claws and little toes. The tiny mews were endearing. She could sense more in the mother cat's eyes and knew she could kill one with a swift move of her hands if necessary, but she was not afraid of the odd animal.

Ainia was fascinated, and Mel let her hold a kitten. She cautioned her with, "Gentle now, be careful." The unsteady girl was seated on

the floor of the kitchen and gently touching the soft kitten. When it mewed, she looked up in wonderment. The mother cat looked to see if the kitten was in distress and then closed her eyes to slits in contentment as the kittens suckled.

"Okay, let's give the baby back to its mama," Mel said after Ainia had petted it for a while, but getting the kitten away from Ainia would prove to be more difficult than that. The little girl was not used to being told no, and finally, Alinta had to take the protesting toddler outside while Mel put the kitten to its mother's teat and left them alone.

"I been giving the momma cat a drop of cow's milk. I hope that's okay?" Betty confessed, wondering if she had overstepped. Mel was a big man and intimidating to her.

"No, that's a good idea. We want these kittens to grow up strong and healthy, so they can help around the place." Mel mused for a moment, thinking. "I better send for a tomcat in my next batch of supplies."

Betty nodded, not knowing if a response was required but thinking it was a good idea.

Mel moved the furniture where she wanted things placed that afternoon, including putting the master bedroom set in its proper place. She loved the rich woods, rubbing them gently and smelling the polish that Betty must have used on it. It smelled lemony and made her smile, taking her back to one of her earliest childhood memories. She wondered what people used for wax on the Outback? Did they import all of it? That train of thought led to some interesting speculation on her part.

Mel moved on to her study. The large cherry wood desk looked massive in this room. She had to have some help moving it into the space she chose, but it looked impressive when they were done. Its matching chair sat comfortably behind the desk and rolled easily on the hardwood floors. Next, she started stacking the books she had ordered along with some books that Saunders had bought at her request. There were quite a few to read, and she avidly looked forward to the winter months when she would have more time to read. The books looked inviting on the shelves she'd had O'Grady build and which her men had sanded and stained for her. They looked very nice but were basically empty as the books that had arrived only filled a few shelves. She made a note to write to some people that might know something about bees and honeybees as she knew they were important to the crops. This office, or den, would be a pleasant place to read and write letters.

Sitting down at the desk after dinner, she started the letters she'd thought of earlier in addition to responding to the letter she had received from Abigail in England. Apparently, Abigail was considering a move to Australia, and she wanted Mel's advice since she had been surprised to learn of Mel's move to this continent. Mel frowned. Hadn't she made it clear that her move was not voluntary? Mel responded to the missive, wondering about her friend's marriage and her *husband*. She sneered at that word, memories of her past assailing her as she wrote.

"Come to bed?" Alinta asked from the door, and Mel looked up, surprised by the lateness of the hour. She now had a small clock on her desk to show her the time. She wanted a grandfather clock in the

hallway and had added it to the list of other furnishings she wanted her solicitor to obtain for her. She knew he wasn't pleased being her errand boy, but he was also well paid for his services, and she had received a missive from the lawyer's wife hoping Mel enjoyed *her* choices. Mel gleaned that the woman had enjoyed her experience shopping with someone else's money. She made a mental note to write back to the woman and maybe give her the list directly next time. She would include the grandfather clock on the list and describe exactly what she was looking for and hope she could find it.

"Time got away from me," Mel admitted, having done some of the bookwork for the station while wishing all the while that someone else could do that chore for her. She thought about the wool that was well on its way back to Sydney and would be sent to the mills in England. That thought reminded her of Lady Abigail Worthington, and she thought of an addendum to her previous letter. She smiled at her wife, momentarily comparing her to the English woman and realizing there was no comparison. Alinta was earthy, a primitive woman in tune with her surroundings, and she loved the Outback. Mel knew Lady Worthington could never be happy so far from civilization, and she wouldn't allow her porcelain skin to become tanned in the sun. Abigail was a lifetime ago, and Mel dismissed any comparisons. She loved her wife, and she blew out the desk lamp in order to follow her up to bed.

"Spring?" Alinta asked when Mel explained about the mattress. She wasn't used to the softness of the bed although Mel had ordered a firm mattress, asking for specific things that she was certain her solicitor had delegated to his wife.

"Yes, it's a piece of steel that they coil around, so it springs back if you bend it a little," she explained. She was trying to keep it simple since Alinta had nothing to compare it to in her limited experience. "I'll show you someday," she promised as she washed up in the porcelain bowl of the sink in their bathroom. She was pleased that Alinta had adopted this practice too. Mel didn't mind her wife's earthy body odors, in fact they aroused her as nothing else could, but Mel liked clean. While it had been a fight to get her wife to submerge herself completely in water, she seemed to like the benefits that resulted. Mel had unconsciously made love to her wife more frequently when she bathed, and Alinta had learned that these pleasures were something she wanted…a lot. Mel was only saddened that their lovemaking wouldn't result in another baby but thought perhaps, Ainia would be enough for them.

Mel glanced at the bathtub, debating taking a bath tonight, but she was tired from moving the heavy furniture today after the long ride in from their campsite of last night. Knowing she was probably sweaty, she slowly removed her clothes, including the wraps she used to bind her breasts. Her breasts were not that big, but she preferred them to be held in.

"Bath?" Alinta asked, noticing her *husband* getting naked and enjoying the sight. In her eyes, Mel had a beautiful body, and Alinta hoped undressing was a prelude to the lovemaking and feelings that Mel had helped her discover within her body. The first time Mel had used her tongue between the primitive woman's legs, Alinta had been confused, and then, once she relaxed, she had experienced an ecstasy she hadn't known existed. She'd nearly pulled Mel's hair out when she

grasped the back of her head in her spasms. Mel had grinned, wiped the moisture from around her mouth, and then lain on the smaller woman, making her feel surrounded, not only by Mel's bulk but by her love.

"Yes. Would you like to join me?" Mel asked, looking at her wife speculatively and wondering if she would be brave enough. This bathtub was bigger than the other tub in the house, and it was much grander than the bathtubs in the washhouse or the stockmen's houses.

Alinta looked up, wondering if Mel was planning on drowning her in that tub. She had thought about that back when Mel insisted she bathe in the creek long ago. The thought of voluntarily immersing her whole body in water had been repugnant to her. Used to normal human smells, sweat, and dust on her body, which helped ward off the constant flies and other bugs in the Outback, she had hated the feel of her skin when it was clean. It had felt vulnerable and raw, and the bugs had certainly liked it. That Mel liked it too was soon apparent, and she wanted to accommodate her, especially once they became intimate. When her time was upon her, it was especially nice to clean away the blood, and Mel had shown her how to use the rags. Since they were soon cycling together, it was a good cover for Mel as Alinta could wash their rags together. Alinta saw the mischievous grin on her husband's face and was up to the challenge as she removed the man's shirt that looked like a dress on her small frame. She then removed the boots Mel had had shipped in for her, finding them difficult to wear at first, and now, liking that they protected her feet from stones and snakes. She'd especially been impressed when Mel's knee-high boots had kept

her from being bitten by the death adder. It was another white man thing Alinta could admire.

Mel liked knowing that Alinta wore nothing under her clothes…no corsets, no petticoats, no nothing. In winter, she had condescended to wear summer underwear, but she hated the flap on the back, which allowed her to sit and make her stream. She had wetted the material more than once before the toilets in the house were installed. She liked the swishing water in the house toilets that took away the waste, finding it fascinating to watch.

As the hot water came in from the water reservoir behind the stove downstairs and filled the tub, Mel smiled in anticipation. She liked the idea of sitting in the tub with Alinta and maybe washing her hair. Although she had given the woman a hairbrush, Alinta rarely used it on her wild tresses, and Mel liked the wildness of her wife's hair. Her own hair was extremely short, and she kept it that way deliberately. Mel stepped gingerly into the hot water, turning the cold water on a little stronger to avoid burning her wife's skin. When the water was more of an even, warm temperature, she finally turned off the taps and sat back. Her bulk spread out the water, so less water had been needed to fill the tub.

Alinta stepped in and sat in front of Mel. She was not used to hot water at all. Her father had once taken the family to some hot springs, but the hunting was poor in that area, the water smelled odd, and they didn't stay long. Now, the ability to draw hot water from a faucet—a word that had been hard for her to learn—amazed her. Alinta sat back against Mel, who lifted one of her legs and put it on the side of the tub to make room. She realized she liked this feeling of skin on skin.

Mel had sent to Sydney for the soaps she now used, caressing her wife's body with them as she soaped her up. Alinta had been fascinated by the bubbles but didn't necessarily like all the different smells; however, she did like the sandalwood that Mel used on her own body so often.

Mel loved touching her wife's muscular body. She was amazed that the only sign of the woman ever having been pregnant was a tiny pucker in her midriff. Mel's soapy hands ran up and down the woman's arms, feeling the tender skin.

Alinta had never imagined that the caress of another human being could feel the way Mel made her feel. She desired her husband, her arousal almost instant as they lay in the warm bath together and touched. She held off though, enjoying Mel's touch while wondering what else she would do.

Mel soaped her own short hair. She had kept it cut that way for a while, an excuse to use the razer she kept that others might think was for her beard. She'd made a great to-do about soaping up her face daily when others were around on the trip except when there was no water. It only worried her when there wasn't water for days, and she would deliberately keep dirt on her face to give the appearance of a beard. She was never going to shave. She had known women who had to shave due to whisker hairs growing on their faces but not her. She then began to soap up Alinta's tresses, marveling at the texture of the hair between her fingers and using water cupped in her hand as she poured it on them. She wondered if Alinta's tribe all had hair like this or if she was unique. Mel realized she would probably never know that answer as she continued to wash her wife's hair, her fingers digging into the thick, dark hair as she lightly scrubbed along her scalp.

Alinta had never imagined what the feel of having someone massage her scalp would be like. There was no word for *massage* in her native language. No one had ever touched her as Mel did, and she loved the fingers that probed gently and didn't think about the soap that she worked into her hair. Used to seeing matted hair on many stockmen and aboriginal people who didn't brush out their hair, she would have been fine with that. Mel had introduced her to brushing, and while she didn't brush her hair every day, it was often enough that the oils in her scalp came out and made her hair shine and look lovely. Mel had cut Alinta's hair off just below her shoulder blades, so it was easier for her to handle, and she enjoyed it as she had never thought possible. Mel also admitted to enjoying running her fingers through her wife's hair, missing the days when she also had long hair, before that feminine part of her was long lost.

Gently, Mel cleansed her wife's hair and then moved down from there to her lovely shoulders that were so soft. They were no longer dark brown as she had seen them when her wife wore less. She continued under her arms, washing the long hair there and wondering why this too was different from her own. She had discovered that Alinta was ticklish when she washed down her sides and her short legs. Finally, she began to wash between her wife's legs. There was always the temptation to play with the curls that grew there. Instead, she made sure to wash between the folds, anticipating kissing this later. Her mouth was watering at the thought of the taste of Alinta. She even

washed up and down her crack, then back to the front, making sure she didn't miss any fold or soap residue.

Alinta moaned as Mel *accidentally* touched the nub of flesh she hadn't known was there until her husband taught her. She wanted this woman and turned in the tub intending to wash her too. Mel's eyes enthralled her, surprising her with their intensity as she began to wash her. Mel was so white, the tan on her face ending at the collar where her button-down shirts began. She was amazed to see how dark her arm looked against this white skin.

Mel watched through slitted eyes, enjoying the caresses with the washcloth as the water in the tub cooled. They took a long time in the tub, but she didn't mind as her wife was touching her breasts, which seemed to be enjoying the tweaking. They stood up not only from the cold but also from her wife's knowing touch. Mel smiled as she saw the teasing smile on her wife's mouth. She knew exactly what she was doing to her. Alinta moved on to her torso, moving inexorably down to Mel's legs and then between them. Mel couldn't help herself, gasping at the feel of Alinta's hand between her legs and desperately wanting to feel that touch. Teaching Alinta what pleased her had been one of the best things about being married. She had waited for her for so long: first, for her to give birth to their daughter, and then, for them to finally have the privacy she wanted. She was pleased with how willing Alinta had become. They had turned a terrible incident for the young woman into a pleasure that she now eagerly participated in, initiating their lovemaking on more than one occasion.

Alinta didn't stop with the washing this time. She was inspired by the moans coming from Mel's mouth, and wondered if they meant she

could make her come undone. She dropped the washcloth, rubbing between the folds, and Mel spread her legs, giving Alinta access as she played. Alinta lifted one leg, placing it alongside her own hip in order to get closer. Her fingers slipped inside her lover, and she watched her reaction.

Mel's head fell back, and her other foot reached out, stretching as the sensations began to build and her body began to tense. Unknowingly, she hit the plug on the tub, and it began to drain. She had no idea as Alinta began to work her body, leaning down over her to suckle and tease at the erect nipples that begged for attention. This had startled Alinta at first, who had thought that nipples were only for feeding babies. Learning that pleasure and pain could be derived from this action, she had greatly enjoyed the pleasure and was pleased that Mel gave her plenty of it. Mel wouldn't suckle at Alinta's nipples, leaving the milk for their daughter. The child was precious to her; she had said so many times.

As Alinta's hand fell into rhythm—in and out, her fingers slipping in the wetness Mel was generating—she watched, looking up from where her mouth was working the woman's nipple and hearing Mel's breath catch. Slowly, she played with the larger woman's body, in and out, in and out, and she was pleased when her thumb hit the flesh that stood up slightly from the fold. It was merely a bump, but it was so tender and sensitive that Mel was soon thrashing in the tub. The water was gone from the tub as she came twice, her body becoming tense, then supine, then tense again, and her toes curled as she gasped out a final orgasm, her mouth set stubbornly closed, so her moans wouldn't echo in the bathroom's confines.

Mel slowly opened her eyes. She had not expected her wife's tender touch to turn so erotic. She smiled as Alinta rose from where she lay on her husband's body, giving her warmth in the aftermath of their lovemaking.

"That was…unexpected," Mel murmured softly, feeling emotions she couldn't put into words as she gazed down into the earthy woman's face.

Alinta looked at her earnestly. "Okay?" she asked. That one word said so much, telling Mel that her wife worried that she had done something wrong.

Mel cupped her wife's face, pulling her up her body and kissing her passionately. She wished she could turn over within the confines of the tub. She wanted to cover her wife's body with her own, press down, and take her. Instead, she kissed her passionately, telling her without words that it was more than okay. Slowly, she opened her mouth, her tongue coming into play. Teaching Alinta how to kiss using her tongue had been fun. She was an avid apprentice, and now, her kisses were an intoxicant that could be Mel's undoing once again, if she wasn't careful. "Let's go to bed," Mel murmured, intending to take her wife in bed, perhaps more than once. Her body was already feeling aroused again as Alinta rose and smiled cheekily while carefully getting out of the slippery tub. Mel got up, and the water that had built up behind her bulk suddenly sloshed towards the drain. She cupped some of it to wash her privates once more before getting out of the tub. Her wife handed her a towel, but Mel only superficially dried her body before capturing the wild woman in her arms and kissing her again, then lifting her up and carrying her to their bed.

CHAPTER NINE

Mel slept well, and when she heard Ainia during the night, she was surprised when Alinta didn't hear her too. Alinta had the senses of a wild animal, but Mel knew she had exhausted her lover with their love play, so she wasn't concerned when she didn't awaken at their daughter's cries this one time. She rose, wrapping her robe tightly around her. The robe had come from Sydney, and it fit her well. It was made of a material that didn't cling to her frame, which allowed her to wear it without her wrappings on her breasts. She tied it off as she went to get their daughter, finding her crying in the room they had set up for the baby. There was a matching crib in their room too. Mel had O'Grady make two of them. She was grateful the little girl hadn't been in their room the previous night. She shushed Ainia, changed her, and washed her lightly, so the urine that had cooled her didn't remain on her skin. She changed Ainia's damp clothes and wrapped her in a blanket, but the poor little girl was still restless, and Mel knew this meant she was hungry. Mel was going to have to wake Alinta. She was sorry that she couldn't feed their daughter.

As she walked into their bedroom, she closed and locked the door, then looked at Alinta in the light of the lamp she had left on low on the table beside their bed. The serene look on her wife's face reminded her of the lovemaking they had participated in earlier and made her smile. She looked calm and peaceful, and if she felt as good as Mel had, she needed to sleep. Ainia squirmed, reminding Mel that the baby needed to be fed. Alinta was still naked, and Mel wondered if she could manage to feed their daughter without waking the woman. She slowly crawled into their bed, angling the baby towards her wife's exposed and obviously full breast. The child latched on with an enthusiasm that made Mel cringe. That had to hurt, but her wife never flinched. Instead, her breathing changed, and she slowly woke up and looked down at their child in surprise, then back up at Mel. She smiled as she snuggled the baby closer to her. Her hand reached out, caressing Mel's arm in remembrance of their earlier intimacy. Mel loved this moment so much she could have cried. She hoped she would remember it forever. She watched as the baby suckled, and when she was finished with the one breast, Alinta made to sit up, but Mel stopped her.

Taking the baby, she whispered, "Roll over and scoot onto this side," indicating where she was getting off the bed. She carried Ainia around the bed and got back in, scenting the wet spot that had dried with her wife's amour. They repeated that position, tucking the baby in against Alinta again. The baby wasn't as hungry anymore. She was

more content with a nearly full stomach from the first breast. She soon began dozing off, occasionally sucking but falling asleep again each time. Mel picked Ainia up and put her against her shoulder, patting her back gently to help get the bubbles up. As she looked around the large master bedroom, Mel realized it was missing a rocking chair, and she made a mental note to add that in her letter to Saunder's wife. She would make believe she was asking for *someone* on the station, who had a baby. She had to be careful not to mention her wife to either Saunders, his wife, or anyone else in Sydney, who had known Melissa Lawrence.

Finally, the baby was burped and asleep again, content for the moment. Mel picked her up and placed her gently in the crib, laying her carefully, so if she spit up, it wouldn't choke her. It had taken several explanations to Alinta before she stopped bringing the baby into their bed, even when they were lying on the floor. Explaining that sometimes, people rolled over in their sleep and squashed the baby, she had finally convinced the inexperienced mother to keep the baby nearby in a box, so she wouldn't roll anywhere, especially as she got older.

Alinta had never known a man to take care of a baby. She knew that Mel was not a physically a man, but even the male spirit within her seemed to know how to take care of the baby. Alinta was pleased that Mel thought of the baby as "theirs." The men among Alinta's people were more interested in boys and only once they were a certain age and out of swaddling clothes. Of course, living in the desert, there hadn't been many swaddling clothes. The women preferred to hold the baby out in front of them as they strode along. When the baby pooped or

peed, they would pull on leaves to wipe the baby and keep going, never needing to stop for these duties. This was a natural process, and they didn't give it another thought. White men and women seemed more concerned about their modesty.

Mel returned to their bed, discarding her robe and glancing to reassure herself the lock was engaged on their bedroom door before turning down the lamp and getting into bed with Alinta, then curling up against her frame. She thought of making love to her again but knew they had too much work the next day and couldn't afford to be that tired.

Mel woke slowly that morning, sensing before she reached out that Alinta was gone from their bed. She was a lot quieter than Mel could ever hope to be. She lay there a moment, listening and realizing that the birds tweeting their morning calls were a lot louder than her wife would be. She also realized Alinta had taken Ainia with her. When she got up, she also saw that their clothes had been scooped up to be washed. She reached for a wrap to bind her breasts and began to pull on a shirt, pants, socks, and her boots. She ran a comb through her hair for form's sake. Here in the house, she didn't trim it very often, allowing it to grow longer. Satisfied with her morning ritual, she used the bathroom and noticed that Alinta had hung up their towels and opened a window to prevent mustiness in the enclosed room. The mosquito netting on the window was a godsend, keeping out the eternal bugs that would have swarmed into the house.

Mel headed downstairs to a hearty breakfast, pleased that her wife and the maid had it hot and ready for her. She ate well and went outside, watching the sun come up in the east and feeling pleased with her life. She had everything she never knew she always wanted and needed, and life was good. Alinta joined her.

"What do today?" she asked.

"What are we going to do today?" Mel repeated, correcting her. She tried to teach her wife to speak better English. "Today, we are going to start some bridges."

"Bridges?" Alinta asked, unfamiliar with the word.

"Yes, bridges. We need a couple bridges over the creek for when the rains come, so we can get to the paddocks we are building."

Peter Winston, coming up to the house for his daily instructions, caught that statement and smiled. "Want me to gather some men and get started?"

"Yes, and we must make the bridges the shape of an arch. If anyone knows how, they should speak up; otherwise, we are going to learn by trial and error," Mel said with a smile as she looked down on her head stockman and walked off her porch, nearly tripping on a puppy that had escaped the barn. "We also need kennels for these little guys," she said, scooping up the young dog. Just then, one of the bitches came trotting from the barns. Hearing her pup's cry as Mel scooped him up, she increased her pace to a run. Mel put the pup back down before her, and the dog thoroughly sniffed it before picking it up by the scruff of its neck. The pup went totally limp, and the mother trotted back

towards the barn where a bed was made up in one of the stalls for her and her mischievous pups.

Peter laughed as Mel began describing what she wanted. She was followed by Alinta, who veered off towards the chicken coop to collect eggs with their little girl. Mel was feeling expansive today, and her hands gestured enthusiastically as she elaborated on her ideas.

By noon, several men had helped fell trees and begun creating a bridge that would connect the two sides of the track over the creek. They chose a spot where the ground wasn't worn down by the mass of animals that had trod through the water from the track. Instead, they started it well back from the edges of the creek, knowing it would flood all out of proportion in the rainy season and inundate the track. Mel had explained her arch idea repeatedly. She didn't want brush and debris to build up under the bridge and catch, creating a logjam and possibly taking out the bridge they were working on so hard. It took a week, but they finally completed the bridge off to one side of the track, which would eventually turn into this path, but for now, it was not going to be used. They switched their attentions to duplicating their efforts on the other track towards Twin Station.

"God, it's hot," one of the men complained, using a bandana to wipe the sweat from his neck.

"Jump in the creek and cool off," Mel told him. "You all take a half day," she encouraged, backing away when they immediately began to roughhouse in celebration of her suggestion to take time off. She couldn't afford to play like that and have her secret discovered. A wet shirt might reveal that she was wearing a wrap. "You boys have been working hard on these bridges, and you can finish this one up

tomorrow." Several of the men were already pushing and shoving others into the water, which wasn't very deep in the hot, summer weather.

Mel headed up to the main house to the tool shop, taking a couple of axes along to sharpen them on one of the whetstones she had had shipped in. She liked that they had a pedal to turn the wheel, and she was able to sharpen the tool, which had been dinged and chipped a bit by the hard Eucalyptus trees they had been chopping. Some of the men weren't as handy with an axe, and she was grateful no one had gotten hurt when they occasionally missed the tree and hit the ground near their booted feet or a rock.

As she worked, she thought about the many letters she had written, the responses she had received, and the letters she still had to write. She knew her solicitor was earning his fees, and she had drawn a draft on her bank to pay for his many services in the last batch of correspondence. Opening the track to the southeast had proven to be a good idea as they now had several more folds and eventually, they would have paddocks for the sheep. People could now come to the station, or she could send someone out for supplies, animals, or mail. While keeping her hands busy, she would formulate letters in her mind. After dinner, she would sit down, relax, and write them. Sometimes, Alinta practiced her letters and the writing Mel had shown her. Mel would proudly compliment her as she learned. She really had a sharp mind and only had to be told or shown once before she grasped it. Implementing it was sometimes hard though and had to be repeated or corrected a few times. Still, once Alinta had fully grasped it, she proudly showed off her writing, reading, and speaking skills.

"You gave the men a half day?" Peter came up to where she was sharpening tools, half of them already laid out beside her and ready to go.

"Yes, I felt they needed it, and it is very hot," she said as she continued to ply the pedal and sharpen an axe.

"They're asking for drink," he warned as she began to look at the sharpened tools, turning one or two over.

"Watered down rum is fine, but I don't want anyone getting drunk. We have a lot of work to do, and I thought to allow them this time off for only one day."

He agreed, nodding. "I thought I saw smoke south of here," he warned.

"Grass fire?" she asked, fearing the stories that Fabiola and Harold had told them long ago. They'd been fortunate that they hadn't seen any on Lawrence Station yet, but the men on the tracks, the swagmen who went from station to station and who had just discovered their far Outback station, spread their own tales. Their tales were from other stations, east of their own, and some of them were gruesome. Upwards of tens of thousands of sheep, cattle, other livestock, and human lives had been lost. Mel only doubted a small percentage of the stories. She felt there was a basis of truth in most of what they said. Those on Lawrence Station had been watching, but perhaps, they needed a better system.

"I thought so. It might have been a campfire too, but it would have to be a pretty big campfire to create that much smoke."

"Well, no swagman is going to make a big campfire; they know only too well the dangers of doing that. Only someone

unknowledgeable or afraid of the Outback would do that," she mused, thinking about it. "Better send someone to investigate."

"I'll go myself. I'll take some supplies out to the eastern folds and scout where we will be wanting to put some of the fence lines."

Mel nodded. She had discussed with her men extensively about where she wanted fences to go up on the property. They'd erected markers and stakes, so when the fence builders got that far they would know where to place the fence lines.

CHAPTER TEN

Peter set out riding a horse and pulling two pack horses. Resupplying the men every few weeks was a job that they switched off. Mel went when she could, but running the station was full-time work, and she couldn't always get away.

He stopped at the fold nearest to the station, the one that would get resupplied last on the next go-through. He continued onto the second and third folds before stopping for the evening. He discussed with each of the stockmen where they felt the fencing to create their paddocks should go. From taking the sheep out for grazing and moving them, so they didn't overgraze an area, they knew their areas the best and could pinpoint land formations to avoid as well as the best spots to fence off, so the sheep didn't wander. Even the best sheep herder or dogs could lose sheep as they wandered in their search for feed. Dingoes were not their only worry. Some sheep could be very independent, and their herding instinct might not be as profound as others. The Lawrence Station was probably too young for these woolies that other more established stations had. These animals were very adept at fending off predators such as dingoes and keeping themselves alive.

Peter didn't find the remains of the fire he thought he had spotted from the station, but he had kept quite close to the track in order to go from fold to fold and deliver the supplies. He did see a swagman out beyond the fifth fold he visited, who was heading towards the home station. It took a long time for them to meet since the track dipped up and down the hills and gullies.

"Hey there," he greeted the man, who was walking along, his clothes dirty from the dust of the Outback and the now well-worn track. There had been a dust storm in this section a few days ago, so he might have been caught in that too.

"Hey there. Is this the track to Twin Station?" the man asked.

"No, this is the track to Lawrence Station," he corrected, pulling up his horse.

"Lawrence…Lawrence…" the man mused, as though trying to remember where he had heard the name. He shook his head, causing the hat on his head to move and making the things he'd tied with bits of string to the edge of his hat bob. He had tied them to his hat to ward off flies. "What is this Lawrence Station's owner's name?" he asked.

Peter wondered why the man would care. Most of these swagmen were only looking for temporary work, enough to earn their tucker and enough food to get them to the next station. Often, they'd accept the

food for doing nothing. "Mel Lawrence owns the station," he answered.

"Mel?" the man asked, sounding confused but obviously trying to remember the name.

"Aye, Mel Lawrence," he repeated, wondering at the man's confusion.

"Tell me. Is this Mel Lawrence a big man? Six feet, maybe thirteen or fourteen stone? Black hair?"

"Aye, that would be him. You met 'im?" His horse fidgeted a little, sensing Peter's unease.

"Why that–!" the man began angrily. "He cheated me in cards," the man asserted, looking furious.

"Well, I've never played cards with Mr. Lawrence, but I know him well enough to know he wouldn't cheat anyone." Peter wasn't liking this man, but there were all kinds of swagmen out here. Some of them were a little touched in the head and better left alone.

"He owns this station?" his hands took in the track, the land around him, the rolling hills, the trees, and everything.

"Yes, he does claim it, and he has been making improvements ever since he brought the first flocks in here." Peter was beginning to feel defensive, and he didn't know why.

"Why that bugger didn't–" the man started, staring at Peter and then abruptly starting down the trail, turning away, and disappearing into the brush.

Peter started after him but couldn't find him. Knowing that he wasn't a tracker, he dismissed the man as crazy and forgot about him as he resumed his travels to the other folds.

CHAPTER ELEVEN

A week later, several men came riding in hell bent for leather and looking to gather help for a fire in one of Twin Station's northern paddocks. Mel took a dozen men down the track, leaving a call for anyone else who could be spared to head to the fire. She knew that Twin Station would do the same for her if she needed the help. Several stockmen along the way left their flocks with jackaroos in order to follow Mel and help fight the fire. Fortunately, it was a small fire, and they were able to put it out in record time. Mel had gotten a couple burns from sparks, but all the men did, and she accepted the thanks of Carmen and Fabiola, who had been surprised and pleased to see her and her men arrive followed by the others half a day later. Their combined efforts had proven a godsend as they put out the fire.

"It's a dry year," Fabiola commented as Mel used her handkerchief to wipe at her face, squinting at the hot, Australian sun.

"Aye, it has been that," Mel agreed, wondering when she had started using Australian lingo. She had never in her life used aye, except maybe once when she was on board ship, and that was a time she'd prefer to forget. "Any idea how it started?"

"Dry lightning," Carmen put in as she came walking up. She eyed Mel, watching thoughtfully as she rubbed at the soot on her face. Most of the men didn't worry about their appearance as they made sure all the coals were out, burying them with dirt or sand and stamping them out or using sacks to whip at them. During the fire, the sacks had been helpful but running out of water meant that other things were more effective.

"I'm just glad we didn't have to light a backfire, and we didn't lose any sheep," Fabiola agreed, looking at Carmen in concern.

"We'll be heading back to our place," Mel put in. Now that the fire was out there was no reason to linger about. She had left Alinta and Ainia, and she wanted to get back to the home paddock. Gathering their horses, some of which had broken their hobbles in fear of the smoke smell, they slowly got ready to leave. They accepted the thanks of their friends, fellow stockmen, and the station owners. They headed north, traveling back along the track to their own station. She was pleased to see the nearly straight fence line heading off towards the horizon, the builders nowhere in sight.

Mel was grateful to be home and have access to water again. It was drier west and south of the station, and the water sources in the hidden valley might save them if they dried up any further in this hot,

Australian sun. Right now, it seemed that fall weather, rainstorms, and winter weather were a long way off, but they were coming. Being able to lie in a bath and soak the soot out of her pores was relaxing, as was having clean hair again. There were luxuries Mel knew not many station owners indulged in or could afford, but she needed them, and when Alinta joined her in the tub, it was just that much more enjoyable.

The heat was bothersome, and no one really wanted to work in it, so the best times to work were early morning or early evening. The women kept the gardens intact using water from the creek, but that was getting dangerously low. The livestock were watered in the morning and evening, and this was also the time that predators like the dingoes hunted, so it was a dangerous time. Snakes sought the coolness as well, and Mel constantly warned her men to be on the alert. She didn't want to lose any of her workers, and she also couldn't afford to lose livestock. She'd invested a lot in this station, perhaps more than she should have, and she hadn't realized a profit yet. Both her accountant and solicitor had written her and warned her she was over-extended. Neither of her Australian factors knew about the funds she had in America or England, but then, she had also drawn much against those accounts, and she wanted to repay those funds.

The heat continued to intensify, and Mel worried that the metal roofs had been a bad idea. They were getting so hot that she wondered if they could burn through the wood underneath. She watched the skyline constantly for signs of rain. Any breath of fresh air or cooler air was avidly welcomed. Instead, they only got dust storms. Great clouds were billowing across the land and choking everything in their path. Mel listened to the sand as it blasted against their buildings. She hoped no one was out in this mess, although she and several of the men had made their way to the barns to take care of the stock and gather the eggs in the poultry pens. She joked that the sand would penetrate the eggs. Mel wouldn't allow Alinta or Ainia out in this weather. Alinta seemed amused at her concern but did as Mel asked since it was a request and she hadn't demanded it or commanded it.

Mel found that slipping over the edge of the trail into the valley sometimes gave them a little relief from the horrible, hot winds. The animals that grazed in this area of the station were lucky. The dust didn't completely miss the valley, but it did come down at an angle, leaving a section at the beginning of the valley free of the choking dust and winds.

Nothing and nowhere was completely safe from the winds or dust. It built up everywhere and in every crevice. The wind found any gap between the wooden boards and blew dust through it. No matter how often Betty dusted the main house, within hours there would be another coating of dust. They kept the windows and doors shut, but that just made everything stifling. Only the basement seemed marginally cooler, and Mel had Alinta take Ainia down there to play among the supplies stored there. For once, Mel envied Betty her sleeping quarters, and when the storms continued, they eventually put a mattress on the floor and slept down there, so they could breathe.

The hot winds that blew in between the dust storms only dried everything out further, and Mel had one of the boys stationed in the cupola on top of the station house, which gave him a three-hundred-sixty-degree view to keep an eye out for smoke or dust storms. She had opened the windows and leaned out to wipe down the glass, which would allow them to see through it clearly. She entrusted the watcher with her telescope, which allowed him to see much farther than he could with the naked eye. She advised him the value of the apparatus and warned him to use it carefully. She watched as he was at first, amazed, and later, a bit playful with the telescope. Again, she reminded him of its cost, and he showed more respect for it.

They were able to quickly stop a fire from a small heat lightning strike in one of the paddocks they had managed to enclose nearer to the home paddock. They had also enclosed acreage where sheep could be housed temporarily when they came in to be sheared. This heat lightening was dangerous as the clouds that brought it gave them the hope of rain they desperately needed and yet it could strike from miles away; it was very deceptive.

Mel returned from this small fire dusty, disheveled, and looking forward to her bathtub. She hoped they had enough water in the well, so she could have a good, long soak, but she was willing to take a smaller bath with a pan if necessary.

"Mr. Lawrence, sir?" Willie asked, his voice breaking as he emerged from the cupola where he had been keeping watch. The telescope was held firmly in his hand. He knew how important it was to watch for fires, and the cupola was one of the highest points. He kept watch, making a game of it and using the telescope in sweeping arcs around the countryside and over the hills, even spying on people down along the creek sometimes.

Mel handed her horse off to one of the other boys, who was being trained as a groom. She slapped at her clothing with her hat to remove some of the soot and dust. She looked up at the boy, hoping he didn't have bad news for her. She needed a bath and some sleep very badly. She saw Alinta was on the porch with Ainia and the kittens, who had been growing quickly. Keeping these kittens alive until they became adult cats was important to Mel. Between the snakes, the dingoes, and their own dogs, it was going to be difficult, but they'd kept them in the house for the most part. The kittens were getting too old to have this many in the house, and they soon needed to be moved out to the barn. "Yes, Will. What is it?" she asked him.

The young man liked that. Mr. Lawrence always called him Will while everyone else called him Willie. Being called Will made him feel older than his twelve years. "I saw something, and I don't know if I should tell you or not?"

"Is it a fire? A storm?" she asked him with some urgency.

"No, sir."

"Then, can it wait?"

Willie hesitated for only a moment as he thought that over and then nodded. "Yes, sir."

"Good. I need to shave and clean up," Mel said, and for emphasis, she rubbed her jawline and her imaginary stubble. She glanced at Alinta, who smiled to see her and exchanged a delighted look with her wife before focusing on their daughter, who stood up and said, "Pa!"

"Hang on there, darling," Mel warned, putting up her hands. Her grubby clothing was something she didn't want to taint her daughter. Alinta stopped the toddler from rushing Mel and laughed as the child strenuously objected.

"You get any tiffin?" Mel asked Willie, using the Australian word for supper or dinner, depending on the time of day.

"Yes, sir. Missus Lawrence makes sure I get me grub twice a day," he assured her.

Mel smiled. She still loved hearing that missus part. "That's good. I'm going up to bathe," she announced to both Alinta and Willie. "You better get back to watching for smoke and dust," she told him and watched as he scampered off.

"You okay?" Alinta asked, glancing at the fatigue she could see on her husband's face.

"I'm good. Could use some water though," she admitted as she moved to go inside. "Anything wrong with the well?" she stopped to ask, looking at her wife questioningly.

"Down some," she admitted. "Take bath," Alinta ordered with a grin, her white teeth looking very bright against her dark lips.

Mel returned the smile before nodding and heading inside to the stairs. She could see where Betty had tried to dust the stairways with its fine balustrade and handrail. O'Grady had done a fine job building it, and it looked newly polished. There was dust elsewhere from the dust storm four days ago, but she could see Betty was busy in her library and trying to get it off all the shelves. Dusting was an endless job these days.

Mel luxuriated in a lukewarm bath and soaked away the dust and debris that had gotten in her wrap and under her collar. Washing her hair, she thought about the past couple days and worried about her own station. It was wonderful to change into clean clothes, and she carried the dirty clothes downstairs where Betty took them from her.

"How do you like working here, Betty? Are you okay living in the Outback?" she asked as she ate the meal that the maid had put together for her. She leaned back in her chair as she addressed the industrious young maid.

"Oh, I like it fine. I wasn't sure at first, but it's right fine," she admitted shyly. "I've been stepping out with one of the men. He be a courtin' me." She smiled.

Mel had known that and foresaw that they would have to build more stockmen's houses eventually as more of the men either took wives or sent for their wives. There were quite a few that would be lifelong bachelors and didn't mind living in the barracks with the others. These men preferred the companionship of other men, and she even knew of one set of bachelors who might like to set up housekeeping on their own. She was waiting for just the right time to discuss it with them. It wasn't like when she was back on the ship, and she certainly respected the men's privacy on this subject. Maybe they could take one of the flocks to one of the paddocks she was planning.

"And the work? Should I be looking for a cook or another maid to help you?" Mel asked.

"My work okay, sir?" the woman suddenly sounded worried.

"Yes, it's good, very good. I just see how hard you work for us, and I don't think it's fair for you to do all the cooking and cleaning. Maybe we should be training some of the younger girls. Maybe they would like a chance to become a maid and work under your guidance?" she suggested.

Relieved, the maid thought about it, wondering if she was too young to be training anyone. "I think that may work," she responded.

"Would you have any objection to training any of the aboriginal girls that might apply?" She watched the maid carefully as she asked.

"No, sir," she said right away, and Mel had to wonder if the girl had been giving this some thought all along.

"This is a good meal. Would you like to be a cook?" she asked with a wry, little grin, remembering the first few times she had tried to teach her wife to cook. Alinta wasn't as good on the stove as she was over a fire, complaining that the stove was too big.

"Oh, no, sir. Not a cook. I's mean, my ma taught me to cook and such, but I prefer my maid duties."

"So, housekeeper is what you attain to?"

"Oh, yes, sir…someday," she said with an excitement in her voice that Mel knew wasn't feigned. She knew she was far too young to get the title now, but her ma would be so impressed when she finally earned it.

"Well, then, we'll ask the girls down on the creek if any would like to be an under maid and learn how to take care of a house," Mel announced. "Think you can interview them and see if they'd be any good?"

"Me?"

"Well, you'd have to work with 'em and train 'em," Mel told the surprised young woman with a grin.

Betty thought about it for a moment and nodded slowly, agreeing. "Yes, sir."

"That's settled then. I'll ask the girls and let the word get out that they need to come see you. If any don't work out, that's for you to decide. I think I'll write my solicitor for a cook for the household. I just didn't want you to think it was a reflection on your duties. You've been doing a fine job," she assured the young woman.

Mel took her dishes to the sink, but the girl was already there to take them from her and begin washing them right away. Mel left to join Alinta on the porch, swinging Ainia around and delighting in her squeals of laughter. "How have you been, luv?" she asked her wife, pleased to have this time alone with them, even if it was only for a few minutes.

"Hot," Alinta understated, fanning herself as she sat on the porch in the shade in a chair one of the men had made. There wasn't a breath of fresh air, and she'd soon take Ainia inside to get her out of the heat even though the house was stifling too. Still, the basement was marginally cooler, and it would be better to take her down there.

Mel chuckled but agreed with her wife, glancing towards the west and hoping the clouds she saw there were rain clouds and not just building up to bring more dry storms.

"So, I sees this man on the track, but when he sees riders from the station he goes into the brush and hides. I don' see 'im for a while, and

when I spots him again, he is closer. I think he went along the track in the brush but out of sight."

"Did he come up to the paddocks? Did he find Peter and ask to get hired on?" Mel asked Willie, who was finally reporting what he had seen.

"No, sir. I ain't seen him again at all. Then later, I thought I caught a glimpse of him again, but he went back into the brush."

Mel frowned at that. Many of the swagmen were eccentric, and she hoped he was just taking his time about making an appearance. She looked down towards the track that Willie had indicated as the sun was setting. The heat hadn't lessened, and there were shimmers of heat as she gazed out on the horizon. "Okay, Willie. You better head home for the day, or your ma is going to think you live here," she teased. She smiled as the boy ran off down the hill heading for the stockmen's houses along the creek. She glanced to where men were working around the barns and sheds, shoveling sand from inside them or around them. Since it was marginally cooler with the sun setting, she had told the men they were only to work during the morning and evening hours rather than anyone becoming ill from working in the hot, afternoon sun.

"We better get some rain soon, or the sheep will be dying off," Peter said as he came up to talk to her.

"Anyone hear from the folds?" she asked, tired from her own day and about ready to head in to bed.

"Nothing we aren't expecting; graze is down everywhere. One of the men reported food missing, but he may have been mistaken."

"Food went missing from his hut while he was out with the sheep?" Mel asked.

Peter nodded. "I think he just wanted more than his fair share of rations," he chuckled, and Mel smiled.

Thinking, Mel suddenly asked, "Was it one of the folds on the way towards the track to Wilcannia?"

"Aye, it was. Something important about that?"

Mel told Peter about the man Willie had spotted with the telescope. "He may just be checking us out before approaching, but maybe he got some extra supplies while the stockman was out with the sheep?"

Peter nodded, and he too looked a little concerned. Receiving no further instructions, he bid Mel good night and headed back to the barracks. He was one of the stockmen who was sending for his wife and children now that he had the lay of the land out here on the station. With his position as head stockmen secure, he now wanted his family about him. It would be safest if his wife and children traveled with the supply carts that would come after the rainy season. Mel had written the letter for him since he didn't know how to write, and the arrangements were made. He was looking forward to seeing his family.

The next day, they were all pulled from their beds as Willie pointed a finger at the smoke that was starting to the southwest. They rushed putting tools in the carts, many of the men climbing on quickly to go put the fire out before it really got started.

"This weren't no natural fire," Peter pointed out to Mel as they finished the clean-up. The fire had only burned a couple of acres, but it could have been much worse, and they all knew it. It was a good thing Will had spotted it and they'd been prepared with the cart full of tools.

"You mean it was deliberately set?" Mel asked, concerned.

Peter showed her where the fire had started and pointed out there was no ring of stones that most people would know to lay, and a campfire that had been left to burn.

"Who would do this?" Mel asked, alarmed.

"Someone who wants to burn you out?" Peter asked, wondering at the strange man they had spoken of the night before. "I met an odd character a couple months back on the track..." he began and told her about the swagman, who had been angry when he learned Mel's identity as the owner of the station.

"Wonder who that could be?" Mel asked.

"I don't know, but he seemed like an odd one. I didn't tell you about him because I assumed that was the end of it when he disappeared into the brush."

"I wonder if it's the same man Willie spotted." Mel was pondering who might have such a grudge against her that they would start a fire deliberately...someone that would jeopardize not only her station but the many people working for her, their livelihoods, and the livestock. "See if you can track who did this, Peter. Ask the Aborigines if any of them are trackers. I want to know who did this."

Peter nodded and went to his horse to start casting about.

CHAPTER TWELVE

The fear of fires was lessened the next week as some of the clouds sent them rain, but it certainly wasn't enough. It wasn't anything like the downpours they had gotten in the past, but it was too early for the rainy season yet. It seemed like more rain had fallen on the southern pastures, and Mel was surprised when she saw Carmen and Fabiola coming down the track one day.

"Well, hello there. Out pleasure riding on this fine day?" Mel teased as she looked up from where she was repairing the paddle on the wheel that pulled water onto the garden. Alinta was nearby gathering vegetables, and she looked up, shading her eyes despite the hat.

"Believe me, I wouldn't have made that ride just for pleasure," Fabiola told her as she got down from her horse. It was one of Carmen's fine blacks, and Mel admired it.

"We have a present for you and wanted to discuss something," Carmen said as she came forward with a young stallion that was a fine imitation of her stallion, Dancer.

"*Oh, Carmen,*" Mel said reverently, taking the rope she was offered with pleasure. She immediately let the young stallion sniff her and get used to her scent, then reached up to pet the fine, young beast.

Carmen smiled, pleased with her friend's reaction. Mel had paid for this horse a couple years ago. "I haven't named him, but the vaqueros are calling him El Diablo." She waited to see if Mel knew what that meant.

"The Devil?" Mel asked and started laughing at Carmen's nod.

Fabiola was relieved, in more ways than one. This youngster was causing trouble in their home paddocks and had to be kept well away from Dancer, who already sensed a competitor for his harem of mares. Already, they had had to rebuild two of the new stalls that O'Grady built for them because of Dancer's temper tantrums and attempts to get at this young buck. It was for that reason and others that they had decided to make this trip.

Mel reverently started patting the horse, loving his conformation and proud head that came up to look around. She examined him thoroughly and smiled at the bargain she had made so long ago. As a two-year-old, she might not be able to breed him…but then Carmen interrupted her train of thought.

"He is game, he is," she told her. "I'm not so sure he hasn't already covered one or two of my mares, and I thought it was time to bring him home." She blushed slightly at the indelicate subject, but she was a horse rancher in part, and this was a natural part of the process.

"I'm glad you did," Mel told her as she gazed at the fine specimen. Even after coming all the way from Twin Station, he looked fresh and willing to go on for miles. A two-year-old already covering mares? She shook her head. The stallion she had gotten with her herd of mares was not going to be happy. "Let's get him into his own stall, and you can tell me why you made this long trip. A groom could have brought this happy boy," she crooned to the horse, trying to befriend him. He was eyeing her and switching his tail but not only at the flies that plagued them all.

"Hello, Alinta," Carmen said, giving the aboriginal woman a hug with one arm, pleased to see her. "Where's that precious daughter of yours?"

"She play in the mud," she said, pointing to where Ainia was playing happily with dirt. "No, no, don't eat," she warned the toddler, going back to pick her up.

Ainia noticed the horse, which was obviously younger than the others. She looked at the strange women staring at her and went to put her filthy fingers in her mouth. Alinta stopped her and Mel laughed.

"We keep her close with snakes and other things about."

"I had to hire a nurse to help Maria and Gabriella keep track of my children," Carmen lamented. "I think I need bridles on those boys."

Mel laughed as she was supposed to, her attention back on the young horse. "Come on up to the house, and we'll get you settled. You're staying the night, aren't you?"

"Yes, but only the night. We have to get back," Fabiola warned her, walking behind the large woman with her own horse.

"Alinta, do you want to ride on the horsey?" Carmen offered.

Mel suddenly realized Carmen wasn't riding her beautiful stallion, Dancer. "Where is Dancer? Is he okay?"

"I had some of our men hold him back, so this young upstart, El Diablo, didn't start something. He has bad manners sometimes," she said, her delicious Hispanic accent making it sound intriguing. She gestured to the men that were inspecting the bridge Mel and her men had built at the beginning of the season. It was high and dry and looked ludicrous sitting there over the trickle that was now their creek.

Mel laughed again, pleased with the naughty young stallion as she walked up the hill, her guests following her and her wife following them while holding onto the dirty Ainia, who was clapping her muddy hands together causing even more of a mess.

Ainia was handed off to Betty once Alinta washed her up, and the little girl went down for a nap with almost no squawking. Mel fixed watered down rum for her guests, and they all sat on the porch of the house. The vaqueros that had accompanied their senora were heading for the barracks and the hall.

"We have a problem," Fabiola began without any airs. "Someone is camping on our land, and he has started a few fires by leaving his campfire, but we've been unable to track him."

Mel exchanged a look with Alinta before she addressed her guests. "We had a suspicious fire too. It was the same thing; a campfire that was left burning. Peter went to track him with the Aborigines but found nothing. He simply disappeared." She told of the man that Willie had seen through the telescope.

"If he's been starting fires, he must be stopped," Fabiola said passionately and angrily. At that moment, Mel could see the Aborigine in her features; she looked fierce and primitive.

"I agree, but one man alone could hide out here indefinitely," Mel pointed out, gesturing to the rolling hills and gullies of the Outback.

"If he's lighting fires, we'll find him," Fabiola promised menacingly.

Mel had to agree. It was beyond irresponsible, and she was alarmed. It wasn't the miles of scorched land that the fires could cause, it was the loss of life that bothered her the most. Her men, these men who had come to work for her, depended on her for their livelihoods. They'd lay down their lives to put out any fire on or off the station and had already shown that with the two skirmishes they'd had.

It was nice to visit with the couple from Twin Station, but when inquiries about Harold were met with diverted conversations, Mel dropped the subject. She showed them the improvements that had been made since the last time they were there, and Fabiola talked Mel into gifting her one of the kittens, whispering that it was for Carmen's female cat, who had been in heat many times with no relief since it had arrived on the station. The male she chose was a thin, black thing, but no one knew the potential in the adolescent kitten. She rode off the next day with the kitten hanging out of her saddlebag, its small face looking out sorrowfully at the odd view.

Mel was uneasy. If they had a maniac lighting fires out there, they all needed to be on alert. She went down to the barracks and made an announcement in the hall about what the Twin Station owners had told her, sharing her own suspicions as well about what Peter had told her about the swagman. "I don't want Lawrence Station to be considered unfriendly, but until this man is caught or moves on, we need to be a little more cautious about swagmen and visitors." She knew visitors wouldn't be a problem as they rarely had any and most were open and friendly. But they needed to be cautious about this man that was hiding.

Alinta was uneasy. She could feel something in the air, and it was like the heat waves that came in droves across the plains. She could sense something, but she didn't know what it was. It made Ainia upset whenever her mother tried to hold her as she could also sense something coming from her mother. Mel was the only one that could calm the toddler, but frequently, she was too tired from hauling water to the stock. The creek was nearly dry, and they were all worried.

CHAPTER THIRTEEN

The fire started in the second paddock away from the station. They all saw the smoke once Willie pointed it out. Everyone headed out to battle it. Mel kissed Alinta goodbye, knowing this was a big one from the cloud that rapidly rose on the horizon. The men, the women, and the Aborigines were piling in the carts to fight the fire that was being rapidly carried along by the heat waves and burning everything in its path.

It was even worse when they got to the scene. The fire was creating weather of its own, making wind swirls that were so hot the trees were exploding. The stockman watching over this fold had stampeded the sheep south and away from the expanding fire. The first few creeks didn't hold the fire since there was no water in them anymore, but a couple of billabongs enabled them to wet sacks and fight the smaller fires and keep them from getting out of control while they lit back fires to combat the main fire. It took them over a week, and even then, the men still found hot spots and wearily stomped them out. Dozens of riders from Twin Station arrived, including Fabiola, Harold, and Carmen. They brought food, supplies, tools, and additional men. They fought side by side with the Lawrence Station people to keep the fire from jumping more creeks and moving farther. As the fire tried to burn west, it encountered the sparse desert-like vegetation, and with fewer things to burn, it died within itself.

"Whew, that was a bad one," Fabiola groused as they washed up, looking towards the sky as thunder rumbled above them. It had taken a week, and they were all tired and grimy.

"Oh, God, please," Carmen prayed reverently, hoping that the storm clouds meant rain. Her prayers were answered, and the clouds that had been teasing them for weeks delivered only a sprinkling at first, then later, a nice steady rain, which put out any lingering sparks. They all washed up and headed to their respective stations. Mel gave her friends a hearty, "Thank you!"

Mel was looking forward to getting home and returning to some semblance of normalcy. She helped the men and women get out of the carts and put away some of the tools. Some of the women wearily headed down to their homes to get out of the wet, filthy clothes they were wearing. The men soon followed once everything was put away. Mel wondered if Alinta would meet her on the porch and was surprised to see she wasn't there. The rain felt fine. It was coming down steadily, and she hoped it wouldn't become a problem and wash away land along the creeks before they had time to absorb the moisture.

"Alinta?" she called as she came into the house, putting her hat on the tree near the door and leaving the door open, so the screen door could let in some air.

"Mr. Lawrence, Missus Lawrence has taken to her bed," Betty came in, leading Ainia by the hand.

"Pa!" the girl yelled, but Mel held her back.

"I've got to wash up, my darling girl. Can you wait with Betty while I do that?" she asked the tot, smiling down at her.

Ainia nodded earnestly, looking at the filthy figure of her father in his dungarees and button-down shirt with the sleeves rolled up. Mel was soaked, but the shirt was dark enough that her wraps didn't show. "What's wrong with Mrs. Lawrence?" Mel asked as she headed for the steps, alarmed and not wanting to upset their little girl.

"I don't know, but she's been sick for nearly a week. She won't eat none, and I can barely get water in 'er."

Mel didn't need to hear any more and began running up the stairs two at a time. She opened the door and a wave of sweat and musty air hit her. She looked at the lump in the bed and made sure Alinta was breathing. She was staring off into air, and Mel went to open the windows and let in the cool, fresh air to clean out the stagnant air of the room.

"What's wrong, darling?" she asked tenderly, looking down at her wife. She had never seen the aboriginal woman ill once in all the time she had known her. Even while pregnant and giving birth there was a hearty constitution to this woman.

Alinta barely looked at her, and when she finally focused on the dirty figure of a man, she nearly recoiled.

"Alinta?" Mel asked, not understanding when her wife cringed from her touch. "Alinta, what's wrong?"

It was her voice that got through to the woman. Alinta blinked, seeing the woman she loved beneath the filth and not the man Mel projected to the rest of the world. Her short hair was full of grime, and her face looked as dark as Alinta's skin.

"Mel? Mel?" Alinta began to sob as she sat up and wrapped herself around the bigger woman.

"Shhh, shhh," Mel crooned, rocking her wife and petting her tangled hair. "What's the matter? Shhh, shhh." She tried, but it was a good twenty minutes before Alinta finally stopped sobbing and hiccupping. Mel got up and closed the door, locking it. She fished a handkerchief out of the dresser and handed it to her wife but only after she carefully wiped the tears from the woman's face. "Are you better?" she asked, worrying about what would cause crying like this. Alinta never cried. "What's wrong?" she asked next, seeing her wife was *not* better.

"Man...man..." Alinta hiccupped and cried a little more into the handkerchief, realizing some of the grime and dirt from Mel had gotten on her face and was now on the bed.

Mel could smell the sweat on her wife and worried that she had caught some sort of tropical disease. There was no doctor out here. They did the best they could when someone was hurt. She didn't know what was wrong with the woman, and it was breaking her heart that she was still crying, although it was much less than the torrent of tears earlier. "Tell me slowly. It's okay," she said, trying to take her wife's hands in her own grimy hands. She wished she could wash, but she had to find out what was wrong with her wife first. She was obviously distraught.

"Man, he come, he come," she said, unable to get out much before she started crying again, and then Mel noticed she looked ashamed.

"A man came to the house?" she asked, beginning to be afraid for her wife. It was then she noticed the fading finger marks on Alinta's neck. "What is that?" she asked, reaching to touch them below the nightgown her wife was wearing. Alinta rarely wore the nightgowns Mel had bought for her, preferring the men's long dress-like shirts or going naked in their bedroom.

Alinta flinched away, but Mel's finger caught on the neckline and pulled it away, revealing more fading bruises.

"Oh, my God," Mel exclaimed as she pulled the blankets back. She pulled up the gown and revealed more bruising on her wife's body. "Is your body like that all over?" she asked, horrified at the implications of what had happened while she was gone and unable to protect her wife.

Alinta tried to cover herself, pulling her knees up under the gown and pulling it back down over where Mel had looked. She looked away, ashamed as she nodded and started sobbing, but it lacked the intensity of before.

"Did he…did he…?" Mel began, but she knew, even without asking her wife. She knew what the man had done. She gathered her wife close. At first, Alinta resisted, but Mel was so much stronger than her, and she needed the comfort of her *husband*, the only person who had ever been gentle and kind to her. Mel held her and rocked her, crying for what had happened to her young wife. Her own tears were dribbling down her face and into her wife's hair. They stayed like this

for what seemed like hours, and Mel finally realized the passage of time from the shadows through the windows. As she gently lay her wife back on the bed, her relaxed body told Mel that she was finally asleep. Mel wondered when her wife had last gotten any sleep. There were dark circles under her eyes, so it had to have been a while. Mel covered Alinta, noting the bruises on her arms and wondering at the man who had done this. She quietly rose and went into the bathroom, closing the door to keep the sound of the water from waking Alinta.

Mel cried some more as she undressed, and she cried as she bathed in the bathtub. She had dreamed of this soak on the ride back from the fire but not like this. She cried even more as she washed her hair and her person but didn't linger as she had planned. Instead, she got out of the tub when she was done. She had to wash the tub out to remove the line of filth from the edges, washing the dirt down the drain and wishing she could do the same to the man who had hurt her wife. While she was thinking this thought, she looked at the small bit of soot she had missed and realized the fire had probably been purposely set to draw everyone away from the station. He had known this would leave only a few people to tend to the animals and leave the station vulnerable for the man to commit this savagery. She closed her eyes for a moment, feeling the shame of being unable to save her wife from this.

"Mel?" Alinta called, and she immediately rose from where she had been washing the tub. Grabbing her robe to wrap around her, she opened the door. "I think you leave me," the woman said as the shadows made her look small and thin and very, very tragic.

Mel came to sit on the edge of the bed. "I'll never leave you," she told the woman, taking her in her arms. She could smell the sweat and fear on her wife. "Would you like a bath?" she asked carefully, wondering if Alinta was physically hurt beyond the bruising and not willing to tell her.

Alinta nodded, giving one short, quick jerk of her head, and Mel pulled the covers back again as she carried her wife into the bathroom and set her on her feet. "Wait here. I'll get the water going," she said as she bent over to plug the tub and start filling it again. She gently turned back to her wife, who was looking down at her feet. She lifted Alinta's head with her fingertips. "You are going to be okay," she said firmly, looking into those amazing black eyes and feeling sorrowful.

Alinta nodded again, as though what Mel said was how it was going to be. She allowed Mel to remove the gown, and Mel had to control herself not to shout out in anger as she saw the many bruises all over her wife's body. She wanted details, but at the same time, she knew her wife would probably not want to speak of this ever again. She helped her into the tub and began washing her. Alinta closed her eyes as Mel massaged the soap into her hair, enjoying the familiar feel of her fingers. Mel was careful not to touch the bruises, wondering why some were still so vivid. They looked very painful. She rinsed Alinta's hair and body and said, "Soak in here for a moment. I'm going to change the bed."

Alinta nodded, not saying anything as she lay soaking in the warm water. Mel got up and went into the bedroom. Unlocking the door, she headed for the linen closet and got new sheets and blankets for the bed. She went back in the bedroom and locked the door once again. She quickly stripped the bed, seeing exactly where Alinta had lain for the last week as her body was outlined in sweat on the sheets. Her breasts must have leaked all over the sheets, and Mel wondered how Ainia had been fed while her mother lay in the bed unresponsive. She decided she wouldn't worry about their daughter now; she had looked fine with Betty.

Mel remade the bed, putting the pile of bedclothes in the corner and picking her and Alinta's clothes off the floor of the bathroom and putting them in the pile as well. She got herself dressed, including a new wrap, and fished the other wrap out of the wash, so Betty wouldn't see it. She'd wash it herself and hang it up here in the privacy of their bedroom. Normally, Alinta took care of this for her. Just then, she noted the blood on the dirty sheets. Knowing it wasn't Alinta's time of the month, she wanted to cry for what had been done to her wife.

Alinta was nearly asleep in the bathwater when Mel pulled the plug. She got her up and dried her with a bath sheet, wanting to wrap her in it as she stood there docilely. Instead, she dried her and put a man's shirt on her, hoping that would make her feel better. Mel tucked her wife into the bed, and when she would have left her, Alinta clasped onto her. "Shhh, shhh, don't cry," Mel told her. "I was just going to get you something to eat. Would you like to see Ainia?" she asked, wondering what she could do for her. She didn't know what else to do besides what she was already doing.

Alinta shook her head. "No Ainia," she asserted stoutly as she lay bad on the bed, her wet hair dampening the pillowcase.

"Hold on," Mel said, rising to get another towel and grab the hairbrush from the dresser. She began to brush out her wife's tresses,

something they had both found greatly enjoyable in the past. It took a long time but reminded them both of happier times. The brushing and the bath exhausted Alinta. Mel put the towel down on the pillow and gently eased her wife's head onto it. "You sleep some more," she whispered. "I'm going to get something to eat, and then, I'm going to bring you something to eat. I bet you haven't eaten in God knows how long. Am I right?"

Alinta, responding to the teasing note in Mel's voice, smiled wanly and nodded once as she closed her eyes. She sighed, relieved that Mel was there to take care of her and protect her.

Mel rose and put the brush back on the dresser. In stocking feet, she scooped the dirty clothes in her arms and headed out of the bedroom, closing the door, so Ainia couldn't toddle in if she happened to be up there.

"Mr. Lawrence?" Betty asked as she came down with the laundry. The maid hurried to take it from her.

"Is there any food made?"

"Yes, sir. There's some soup on the stove," she said, wondering what had happened to make Mrs. Lawrence take to her bed. That wasn't like her in the least. Even when her time was upon her and the cramps were terrible, she didn't let anything stop her.

Mel dished up a large bowl of the soup, which was more like a stew, and sat down to eat. She saw some biscuits and dipped them into the filling meal. She knew this was one of Alinta's favorite meals. When she finished her own bowl, she filled another, buttered the biscuits, and put everything on a platter to take up to her wife. Betty watched in worry, wondering what was going on. She'd taken the baby to one of the women, who had a baby of her own. She had stayed behind, so she was able to help breastfeed her. Ainia was with the woman now, but Betty knew the woman would expect her to come and get her soon.

Mel almost had to force Alinta to eat, but talking to her about the new, young horse, El Diablo, drew a smile from her. Except for the eyes, Alinta had teased her that the horse was really a bunyip in disguise. She described to her wife how they'd enjoyed the young horse's antics as he plagued their other stallion and the geldings. He displayed himself to the mares, who watched the juvenile seemingly with humor; however, at two, he was already fully developed, and he'd be even more impressive when he was a three-year-old adult.

Alinta loved the butter-covered biscuits. Butter was something she had never eaten until Mel had introduced it to her. Even cheese out of the kegs didn't compare to the fresh cheese that one of the women knew how to make, and Alinta had avidly learned this skill from her. Not daring to say no to the owner's wife, the other women taught her anything she wanted. As Alinta and Mel talked about anything except what was really bothering the women, she gradually ate. She couldn't eat all the stew as her stomach had shrunk, but she was finally full and sleepy once again. Mel left her dozing again to take the tray downstairs.

"Is Mrs. Lawrence better?" Betty asked, worried.

"Pa!" Ainia called from where she had been messily eating in a special chair Mel had designed to tie her down. She was a wiggly thing, and it was a good thing she had been started on regular food as she mushed the small biscuit Betty had given her into the stew.

"You eat that," Mel told the little girl, who smiled, showing off the teeth she had developed as she tried to push the wet biscuit into her mouth and missed. Mel addressed Betty, "She's getting better." Her look flickered to the upstairs, and the maid realized she meant the missus. "Thank you for taking care of them while I was gone." She tenderly finger combed Ainia's hair as the toddler continued trying to stuff the wet biscuit in her mouth. She was only succeeding occasionally but having a lot of fun trying.

"I don't know what happened. We were all down at the garden, and the missus came up to get some fresh well water for us to drink. She didn't come back, and I found her on the floor in the hall. She was so sick I barely got her upstairs. I found her the next morning in her nightgown, and she wouldn't eat or get out of 'er bed."

"When was this, Betty?" Mel asked as she used a spoon to feed the toddler some of the mashed-up vegetables in the stew. Ainia laughed and ate it gladly. She loved her food.

"A week ago, about two days after you all left for the fire."

Mel nodded. She certainly couldn't ask the maid for some of the more intimate details, not that she would know anything. "How did you all fare while we were gone?" she asked, seemingly innocently as she fed Ainia. By the time the toddler had had enough, Mel had heard enough mundane details and knew the girl hadn't seen anything and couldn't tell her anything more. Mel washed Ainia's face, and the young girl resisted the washcloth angrily.

Mel finished cleaning Ainia up by giving her a bath in the sink and getting her ready for bed. She read to her in her own room from one of the many books Mel had sent for. They included children's books that

she read to both her wife and daughter since Alinta was still learning to read and write. She tucked the toddler in once she had nodded off and closed the door, knowing that she'd yell if she wanted out during the night. Fortunately, she usually slept through the night. Mel was grateful that no one knew what had happened to Alinta. But what if Ainia had been with her? Would the man have hurt the child too?

Mel helped Alinta to the bathroom. Evidently, she hadn't used the bathroom very often in the week she had lain curled in their bed because peeing hurt her. Mel asked to see between her legs and reluctantly, her wife allowed her. Mel saw the slight tears of the skin and tissue, which caused the blood and the pain when peeing. She had a thought. *If the man had raped her wife this way, had he done more?* She couldn't ask her wife and wouldn't probe further. Only another woman could understand how devastating this must be. Only another woman who had been raped could relate. Mel closed her eyes and prayed her wife wouldn't be permanently damaged by this. She loved her so and felt guilty for being unable to protect her.

That night, Mel just held her wife safe in her arms. Alinta, for the first time since Mel had known her, had nightmares. Mel's strong arms around her comforted her when she woke and grasped at her but didn't completely soothe her.

Mel was surprised when Alinta insisted on getting up and getting dressed the next day, despite being weak. Alinta was happy to see Ainia and acted as though nothing was wrong as she resumed her daily chores. Mel watched her and caught her looking cautiously before she went into dark places in the barns and sheds. She wished she could remove that fear, but she could only hover so much. Alinta's milk had dried up, and she slowly weaned Ainia off the woman who had so graciously fed her. They increased her intake of regular food to compensate. Alinta was obviously bothered by the fact that she couldn't provide food for her daughter anymore, and Mel could only watch and sympathize. She didn't understand the special bond between a mother and her babe.

The rain had moved off during the night, but the heat had returned, and a mist hung over the valley as rain that had been absorbed tried to burn off into the air. It was sultry and hot. Mel hated this kind of weather, but the danger of fire was temporarily eliminated wherever this storm had hit. Eventually, more dry weather continued, and another fire sprang up on Twin Station a week later. Mel was reluctant to leave but Alinta insisted, feeling it was time they returned to their work and normal routine. Mel had to take care of her station and help with their neighbors' station, just as they had helped when the situation was reversed. Alinta knew it was time to put the horror of what had happened behind her and forget it. She was alive, and she had her daughter and her husband. She would forget it. At least, that was what she told herself.

This time, Mel made two of the men stay behind and instructed them to keep their powder dry and guard the home station. Surprised, they took their orders as everyone else that was available got into the carts and headed out. Mel mounted her horse, and with one regretful look back at her wife standing on the porch with their daughter, she headed south to Twin Station.

CHAPTER FOURTEEN

Mel fought the fire that was creeping toward the mounded hills that defined the separation of the two stations. She had been working for days, and they all looked hopefully toward the clouds on the horizon. She found herself working with many men from Twin Station that she had never met before. Her own men were off fighting their own sections of the blaze. As she put out some flames using the flat of a shovel, she spotted a man she did recognize. She froze right then and there and stared. She realized who it was, and she realized that this fire, like the others recently, were not from heat lightning. He saw her too and stopped for a moment before dropping the sack he was using to put out flames and sprinting off. Mel threw the shovel like a javelin and tripped him, allowing her to catch up to him.

"You! You is it?" she said angrily. "You did this, didn't you?" She shook him savagely as she picked him up by the scruff of the neck.

"I don't know what yer talking about," Bradley said defensively. Becoming angry, he took a swing at Mel, connecting with her jaw.

Mel had been hoping for that. She immediately let go of his collar and began swinging at the man, not blindly but as she had learned back in New York. She took blows too. The man was a good fighter, but when he tried to grapple with her, the lack of oxygen from the smoke of the fire caused him to weary faster. In that moment, she used her elbow to take out a bunch of his teeth. Furious, he came back and tried to gouge her eyes. She wrapped her arm around his head. "You started that last fire to distract us, didn't you? You couldn't leave her alone!"

"What if I did?" he snarled, trying to twist away from her and slugging at her stomach. Mel punched him squarely in the face, bloodying his nose. "Not like them people ain't used to it. What else are they good for?"

"Hey, what is this?" one of the men called, coming through the smoke to see them fighting.

"Stay out of this!" Mel ordered. "This is the man who set the fires."

Other men heard her, and while they fought the fire, they also watched as Mel began to pound on Bradley's face. When he tried to duck and protect his face, she began to work on his kidneys. "I didn't do nuttin' she hadn't had done before," he told Mel as he spit out portions of teeth from his bleeding mouth.

"Really? You bruised her before too?" she asked. "You're a coward and a bastard," she swore at him as she continued to fight him. Her own lips were cut where they had smashed against her lips, and she could feel both her eyes swelling shut. She aimed a particularly vicious blow to his ear, which affected his equilibrium. Reeling backwards, his arms flailing as he tried to catch his balance, he twirled into a small brush-choked crack along the hillside and landed in a roaring inferno. Mel blinked, unable to move and not willing to save him.

"We've got to–" another man tried to move forward, but Mel stopped him. Her chest was heaving from her exertions, and she was shaking her head to clear the blood from her face.

"He's gone. Leave him. It's a fitting ending for the coward. He started these fires, and he might have killed us all. Go back to fighting the fire. Do what you can," she said kindly, seeing the horrified look on his face created by her words. Mel pulled out her extra handkerchief and wiped her face as the one on her neck had torn off in the fight. She used the small flask of water she was carrying to help wipe away the grime and blood before she too turned back to fight the fire. It was difficult to see through the swelling of her eyes caused by the pounding she had taken from his fists, and the smoke surrounding them wasn't helping either. That was what she told herself as the tears started and ran down her cheeks and nose. She sniffed several times, inhaling the tears, which made her cough along with the smoke. She used the handkerchief to wipe away the grime and tears a few times while she worked to stop the fire.

One by one, the workers came in to eat at the camp they had made as the fire continued to burn. It had been this way for days, and there was no end in sight. The fire had been set in an area that was choked with old brush that probably hadn't burned in decades, and it had

created a wall of flame that marched across the countryside and jumped creeks.

"Are you okay?" Carmen asked, seeing Mel's bloody and bruised face. She'd heard of the fight and death of the man, but she didn't know who he was.

"You remember the drayage company we stopped with on this side of the Blue Mountains?" Mel asked, looking meaningfully at her friend and lowering her voice.

Carmen thought for a moment and then asked, "The one where you gamb–?" she stopped at Mel's nod. They both knew who she was talking about.

Mel explained what had happened with the fight and told how he had confirmed what she suspected about the other fire.

"He was one of the first to volunteer," Carmen explained.

"He would be. He set it, and I'm willing to bet someone nearly caught him. By helping to fight the fire, he hoped you would never suspect him. There are many swagmen who have been helping," she pointed out, gesturing to a couple of them, who were eating nearby. A few were also sleeping and would get up in a few hours to fight the fire where they could.

"What's this?" Fabiola asked, coming up and looking worse for wear with her hair back in a bedraggled bun. "I heard you pushed a man into the fire and killed him?"

"What's that you say? Who said that?" Mel began angrily, but Carmen put her hand on her friend's arm to calm her. She turned to Fabiola and corrected her, telling everything she knew about the man and the fires he had obviously set.

"But why?" Fabiola asked.

"He was after Alinta," Mel confessed. "I won her in that card game, and he always thought I cheated."

"Did you?" Fabiola asked before she could think, and the look she got from both Carmen and Mel quieted her immediately. She made a gesture with her head to show she hadn't meant what she asked. "But to hold a grudge over that?"

Mel mentioned what Peter had seen and what she surmised, putting it all together as she explained everything to her friends. She didn't mention the rape of her wife; they didn't need to know about that.

"I'll put all that in the report I'm going to have to send to the colonial office. You can be sure it will get back to them about the fight you were in and the man's death. The rumors and tales the men tell on the track will be greatly exaggerated, and I don't want anyone coming out to arrest you. As the local magistrate, Harold will have to corroborate the story."

"I'd appreciate that," Mel told her wryly.

"You better get some tucker and sleep," Fabiola suggested. She could see that Mel was exhausted, and the swelling around her eyes meant she wasn't going to be much good to help fight the fire. Fabiola needn't have worried. The rainstorm that had been on the horizon earlier bore down on them that night and put out the rest of the fire, earning a cheer that woke up everyone who had been sleeping or was half asleep on their feet. Everyone came into the camp to eat and sleep, despite the rain. The downpour was nonstop. The next morning, she realized the rainy season had arrived, and Mel was anxious to get back to her station and her wife. Already, the women from Lawrence

Station had packed up the carts, and the men were putting the last of their tools in the carts.

Some of the women had been giving Mel the cold shoulder until Peter told the men that Bradley had admitted he was the one starting the fires, and Mel had stopped him from escaping. During this encounter, Bradley had turned on the station owner and started a fist fight. Peter explained that Mel had only been defending himself and while fighting back, the man had fallen into the fire and was killed. Everyone's attitude changed after this explanation, and the women appeared to be visibly thawing towards the station owner.

Mel thanked Peter as they rode wearily back across the station. The second day, the rain let up, and they spent a less miserable time in the wet saddles as they traveled and dried out, the carts lumbering along the track in the mud.

As they came in sight of the home paddock and used their bridge, a cheer went up among those on their horses and in the carts, and those who had stayed behind cheered in return, welcoming them. Mel thought of it as an omen when the sun came out from behind the clouds and shone on the house on the hill, the barns and sheds, and the massive paddocks beyond them. She saw her wife on the porch of their beautiful house and smiled gingerly, the skin taut and painful across her mouth as Alinta returned her enthusiastic wave.

THE END

✎ About the Author ✎

K'Anne Meinel is the BEST-SELLING author of LAWYERED, REPRESENTED, SAPPHIC SURFER, DOCTORED, VEIL OF SILENCE, SURVIVORS, VETTED and CAVALCADE as well as several other books including her first, SHIPS which was written in 2003 over the course of two weeks. A gypsy at heart, she has lived in many locations and plans to continue roaming. Videos of several of her books are available on YouTube outlining some of the locations of her books and telling a little bit more…giving the readers insight into her mind as she created these wonderful stories. As of this date she has more than 100 published works including shorts, novellas, and novels. She is an American author born in Milwaukee, Wisconsin and raised in Oconomowoc. Upon early graduation from high school she went to a private college in Milwaukee and then moved to California for seventeen years before returning to the state. Many of her stories have Wisconsin in them as settings for her wonderful, realistic, and detailed backgrounds. Named the lesbian Danielle Steel of her time, K'Anne continues to write interesting stories in a variety of genres in both the lesbian and mainstream fiction categories. Her website is www.kannemeinel.com.

If you have enjoyed **OUTBACK SPLENDOR**, I hope you will enjoy

this excerpt from

THE JOURNEY HOME

In the midst of the Great Depression, Cassandra (Cass) Scheimer is trying to keep the family farm afloat in the Big Woods of Wisconsin...alone. As a local midwife and struggling backwoods doctor, she certainly doesn't need more mouths to feed.

Stephanie Evans is a widow enceinte with her third child. She accepts a kind stranger's offer of marriage in exchange for keeping house for him...but he never shows up to claim her. While dealing with unrequited guilt and the desperation of impoverished motherhood, falling in love with Cass is the least of her worries.

For Cass, having been in love with a woman once before, she feels it couldn't possibly happen twice. When it does, Cass is convinced the love cannot be returned. Can she and Stephanie keep it hidden from the prying eyes of children and the meddling neighbors in this small rural community?

Can Cass deal with the guilt she feels over her brother's injury, an injury that prevents him from doing his duty for their country? Joining the Nursing Corps may put too much stress on her newfound relationship with Stephanie. The woman who returns from the war and the woman left behind on the farm are not the same people who once fell in love. Can they return to being lovers after years spent apart? Destiny put them in each other's path, but World War II has them tearing apart.

CHAPTER ONE

She glanced over at the train as it pulled into the station. She never bothered checking her well-trained horses as she unloaded flats of eggs and jars of honey from her wagon. She took large loads up the steps of the store across from the train platform and deposited them at the end of the counter that Mr. Schmidt had indicated. Mrs. Schmidt smiled at the richness and purity of the golden honey.

Cass found it much more convenient to come into town to trade. It was closer to her farm in Merrill, but she did occasionally make the longer trip to Wausau. The traders there were always thrilled to trade her cash money or goods for her rich honey and perfect eggs. Her flats contained normal hen eggs but also, she had duck eggs and huge goose eggs. Some of the shoppers who were lucky enough to obtain these delicacies would be delighted since they made for a richer and more delicious batter when baking or cooking. The goose eggs alone would be worth their price since one goose egg was the size of two hen eggs. This trip Cass also had pelts from fox, muskrat, mink, deer, and rabbit to trade. She left the store richer than she had entered it but also with a bushel bag of flour, one of sugar, a smaller bag of salt, and a few other staples that were cheaper here in the larger town. She packed all this neatly in her wagon behind the seat. She noticed a woman sitting with two small children who must have gotten off the train and was now trying to keep the toddler and older child entertained. They were on the bench before the depot door, obviously waiting for someone.

She got up behind her two horses on the wagon seat and having never set the brake, just spoke to them to get them going. Their ears twitched at her voice and their feet started walking as she expertly turned them around in the wide street before the depot. She backed her wagon up to the loading dock and speaking to the horses again, she wrapped the lines around the unused brake and hopped down. She saw the woman and her children still waiting, but now the older of the two children was crouching down and peering into the crates stacked neatly on the edge of the platform. She smiled indulgently; she could imagine his fascination at what the crates contained. They were why she was here. She went into the depot office nodding with a smile at the woman who watched her son as he delightedly and gently poked his fingers through the slats of the crates.

"I'm Cass Shiemer, I believe those crates outside are mine?" she greeted the depot clerk, her thumb pointing backwards at the stack outside.

"Yes ma'am, I have your paperwork here if you'll just step up and sign. Do you have your letter from the company?"

Cass produced her paperwork showing she was to receive these crates, and their business was soon concluded. She signed for her delivery.

"Can I help you load them, ma'am?" the clerk asked helpfully.

"I'd appreciate it," Cass answered, knowing that she didn't need the help, but one never knew and refusing it would only create a problem.

As she walked out, she was surprised to see one of the railroad men about to kick in the side of one of her crates. The little boy who had been admiring the pups was now cowering against his equally frightened mother on the bench.

"Hold on there, what are you doing?" she asked, alarmed at seeing him intent on harming the crate containing her hard-earned pups.

"That little begger in there bit me!" he said angrily. "I'll teach it some manners." He drew his leg back again.

Cass was faster and ran to pull the leg up. The man lost balance and fell heavily. Everyone heard and felt the crash on the platform. The other crates sent up a squawking and the puppies' startled yipes

"What the hell?" the man yelled outraged.

"Those are my animals, and you hurt them. I'm going to hurt you," Cass said angrily.

"Who the hell do you think you are?" he said ominously as he got up off his backside.

Cass didn't back down as he expected although he towered over her. Instead, she took a step closer and got right into his face looking up belligerently and saying, "I'm Cass Scheimer, and these are my animals you were intent on damaging. Who the heck do you think you are?"

The man raised his hand as though to strike her, and she faintly heard the clerk yelling, "Now, now, she's a lady!"

He looked down at her dressed in men's pants and a flannel shirt covered in a man's dusty coat and matching dilapidated hat. He laughed at the word "lady" and proceeded to raise his hand. It never fell. Quicker than he could blink Cass had a knife pressed to the train officer suit he was wearing. To make her point, she neatly sliced off a button. It bounced and rolled onto the platform.

"Touch me and I'll gut you like a fish," she said pleasantly, never taking her eyes off his as she used her peripheral vision to watch his hands.

Looking deeply into her eyes, he tried to intimidate her but knew with a sickening feeling she was deadly serious. He knew that as a woman, in a court of trial, she would be acquitted on any wrong and he would be found guilty. He reluctantly backed down. Letting out a snort of disgust he said, "A lady," and turned away, shaking his head as he got back into the baggage car of the train.

Cass watched him until he was inside the car and put her knife back in the sheath along her belt. She could see the woman and children cowering out of the corner of her eye.

"Let me help you with those crates Miss Scheimer?" the clerk began warily.

"Who was that?" she asked him, nodding her head towards the empty door of the baggage car. They picked up the crates and placed them gently into the back of her wagon.

"He's new on this line. I don't know where he came from, but he's nothing but trouble," the clerk whispered as they struggled with the awkward crates one by one.

Cass paused after her second load and reached in her pocket for a slip of paper and a pencil. "What's his name?"

The clerk reluctantly gave it to her and saw as she wrote both his and the offensive man's name on the paper. He wondered if he was going to lose his job over this incident. The last crate containing puppies she effortlessly put in the back of the wagon before putting up the tailgate and carefully latching it on both ends. She thanked the clerk for his help and saw the boy watching her again and looking longingly at the crate containing her pups. She grinned knowing how much children loved puppies.

"Cute puppies, aren't they?" she asked him, and he nodded as he took another step towards her wagon to get a better view. His hair had a rooster tail, and it waved energetically in his enthusiasm.

"He was gonna hurt them," he said, glancing at the doorway of the train car the man had disappeared into.

Cass nodded, wondering what the boy was thinking. His mother came to stand behind him, and Cass saw that she was obviously pregnant.

"I wish I could have puppies, someday," he said wistfully. Cass smiled, knowing every little boy's wish.

"Someday, Timmy, someday. Perhaps Mr. Lancaster will let you have one," the woman said softly.

Cass looked up at the name and asked, "Vince Lancaster?"

The woman nodded and smiled. It changed her whole face and made it nearly beautiful. She was small, blonde, and the pregnancy was making her very round. Cass expertly guessed her to be about in her fifth month.

"Do you know Mr. Lancaster?" she asked eagerly.

Cass nodded, wondering what in the world this woman wanted with Vince. "Yeah, I know Vince." Her tone betrayed nothing of how she felt towards the man.

"Have you seen him?" the woman asked tiredly. "He was to meet the train, but business must have held him up."

"Business?" Cass repeated.

"Yes, he must have been held up. I'm sorry, how rude of me. I'm Stephanie Evans, Mr. Lancaster's fiancée." She held out her hand for Cass to shake.

Cass shook it. "You're engaged to Vince Lancaster?"

Stephanie's mouth tightened at the incredulous note in Cass's voice. "Yes, Mr. Lancaster and I've corresponded for some time. In fact, he generously sent the tickets for us to come here to live with him. We were to be married today."

"He know you're pregnant?" Cass asked bluntly.

Stephanie flushed. It was a word that polite company did not use. Most people would have said "in the family way," but not this woman who wore men's clothes and used a knife against a man twice her size. She nodded, "Of course Mr. Lancaster knows I'm with child. I wrote him and told him."

"He get a sight of you?" Cass asked.

"I sent a picture if that's what you're asking." The smaller woman was getting annoyed at this line of questioning.

"Ma'am, I hate to be the one to tell you, but I don't think Vince Lancaster is the marrying kind."

"Why? What do you mean? His letters were most gentlemanly and gallant. He knew of my situation after my husband's demise and offered his comfort, support, and home to my family and me. I sold my home to come here and be his wife," she said almost desperately.

Cass's heart went out to petite, blonde Stephanie, but she knew of Vince Lancaster, even up in Merrill. His reputation was repulsive. If he had been writing this woman, and she was surprised to hear he *could* write, it was for no good reason.

"You knew Vince before your husband's death?"

Stephanie shook her head, and her embarrassment made her cheeks turn an unflattering shade of pink. "I answered an ad that Mr. Lancaster placed in the paper looking for a wife. When he heard of my situation, we began a correspondence."

Cass didn't know what to do. Most likely Vince had gotten someone else to write those letters, laughing at the unknowing woman who had answered the ad. How he had come up with the funds to have her travel here, she didn't know. He never had enough money to drink, much less extra to send train fare.

"Ma'am," she began, and then gulped and began again. "Mrs. Evans, let me take you to where I think Vince might be, and you can make up your mind then."

Stephanie considered for a moment. She couldn't just sit here indefinitely. Timmy and the baby were exhausted, and she realized how tired she also felt. She had to do something. She didn't have a lot of money left after everything had been sold and their bills all paid, but what she did have was precious. She had grasped at the idea of becoming another man's wife, even if that other man was a stranger. Vince Lancaster's letters had been a godsend when she found herself pregnant after Howard's death. A heart attack at 42 was not unheard of, but she never imagined it would happen to *her* husband. When it did, she was alone, with no one to take care of her. Vince's letters had offered her hope and assured her he would take good care of her and her children. In exchange, she would take care of him and his home.

She agreed to Cass's offer to take her to Vince. If nothing else, it would get her closer to him and get the children settled.

Cass effortlessly lifted her trunk into the back of the wagon, proving that she hadn't needed the clerks help with the crates after all.

"We going with her, Mommy?" Timmy looked up at the blonde woman.

She nodded and Cass smiled. "You can sit next to the puppies and keep them quiet," Cass told him. She saw his face light up at the thought. She settled him in the back by the crate with the two puppies inside. She noted their water dish was empty, but the food dish still held some kibbles.

Cass looked at the baby on Stephanie's hip, expertly held by his mother. "Can he be trusted to ride with his brother?" she asked Stephanie. Stephanie looked at the toddler who gazed intently at the puppies with the same rapt fascination as his brother.

"I think Tommy will be fine with his brother," she smiled as he nodded insistently, understanding fully what they were saying.

Cass swung him to sit next to the other little boy and said, "Now I want you two to pet these puppies and keep them calm. This is their first wagon ride, and they are probably a little scared. Think you can do that?" she asked them gently.

Stephanie smiled at how nice Cass was being to her two little boys. They both nodded solemnly. Cass picked up their carryon bags and put them behind the boys for them to lean on. She helped Stephanie up over the wheel before climbing into the front of the wagon to settle herself on the seat.

"Could you hand me that canteen?" Cass asked Stephanie, pointing under the seat. Stephanie moved awkwardly with her girth but managed to reach between her legs and under her skirt for the container.

Stephanie handed Cass the canteen before Cass, in turn, handed it to Timmy and said, "Could you make sure each of the bowls has a little water in it? Don't fill it full because the wagon will spill it, but each of the crates needs a little." She smiled as he nearly nodded his head off in his eagerness to help. "If you're thirsty, you and your brother have a little too, okay?

Cass climbed up effortlessly onto the wagon seat and commanded, "Walk Stanley, walk Stella." Cass turned her attention to her two horses, whose ears twitched, and listening to Cass, began to walk down the street.

Stephanie watched in fascination. The horses hadn't needed the lines that Cass now unwound, and she hadn't even set the brake. The horses had immediately begun upon Cass's command. They drove for several blocks along tree lined streets before Cass spoke again, "Left Stanley, left Stella," and amazingly, the horses turned left at the next street. The streets were decorated with nice houses and a few businesses on the corners, or on alternate streets. They were soon in a part of town not nearly as nice, and Cass pulled up in front of a dilapidated tavern before saying, "Whoa," and the horses stood quietly.

She jumped off the seat and went inside, never looking back at Stephanie or saying anything.

Stephanie stared in amazement at the tavern as though unsure of why someone like Cass would go in such a place. She told the boys to stay in the wagon. They never looked up from the puppies they were petting, their hands shoved between the slats of the crate. She awkwardly climbed out of the wagon and followed Cass. The sight inside wasn't much better with slovenly men with their shirts open, their sleeves pushed up to their elbows and their arms exposed, sitting around stools and tables. They gawked at her attire, her Sunday best. Her eyes adjusted to the dimness of the room and she saw a long bar along one wall and men standing around slurping beer and hard liquor. The smell in the place wasn't much better than its appearance. She set her face as she saw Cass talking earnestly to a tall dark mustached man. He looked like the picture she had of Vince Lancaster. Two other men were listening to Cass unashamedly, and the room quieted as Stephanie came further into it. Every eye went from her to the tall handsome man.

"I told you, I ain't gonna marry her," he was saying and with the silence in the room his voice carried.

Cass noted the silence and looked around in time to see the hurt cross Stephanie's face. The man saw her too at the same moment. His friends smirked and one snickered. Stephanie turned and walked out the door. Cass whirled around and took Vince by the lapels and twisted them in one hand.

"You wrote her. You made promises. Why'd you send her the train tickets if you weren't gonna marry her as you promised?" she hissed angrily. Every ear in the room was listening.

The man tried to get her to release his shirt. It was choking him, and he looked alarmed. "You saw her: she's as big as cow. She didn't tell me..." he began.

"You're a liar," Cass hissed. She pulled out her knife quick as a flash and held it to still his hands from releasing her hold on his shirt. The room was even more silent at that moment. His two friends stopped laughing and looked serious. "You promised to marry her, children and all; you sent her the tickets and made other promises. You're a liar Vince Lancaster, and everyone knows it. You made promises to that woman out there, and she traveled here because of them. For what? A bit of a laugh, for fun? That's fraud. I'm sure the sheriff would like to hear about it." Then she had a thought. "How much money you got on you Vince?" she asked.

He was startled at the change of conversation. The knife unnerved him and he stammered, "A few dollars." he began, but she gave his shirt a twist. "I have fifty dollars," he said. His friends sucked in their breath. That was a lot of money. No one had known Vince Lancaster to have that kind of money, ever.

"You're going to pay the lady for her time and the effort of getting here," Cass told him.

"I already paid for her ticket," he began and then immediately regretted giving himself away with that statement.

"And now you're going to pay for the promises you made her. Pull out your wallet," she held the knife but not in what could be called a threatening manner.

Vince looked around at his friends and drinking buddies, but none of them were going to interfere. At the amount of money he had stated, they had all turned on him. He had borrowed, caged free drinks, and generally free-loaded for far too long on too many for them to be sympathetic. He gingerly reached into his pocket for his wallet and thought momentarily of reaching for the gun, but something in Cass's eyes and the sharpness of the knife told him he would never make it. He opened the wallet and took out five tens; Cass saw there was more in there and said, "All of it!" He handed her the entire sixty dollars as she let go of his lapels but still held the knife. She stuffed the money in her shirt and watched him carefully.

"I'm Cass Scheimer from Merrill if the Sheriff wants to make something of this, but keep in mind Vince, you committed fraud against that woman and I don't think it would go too kindly in your favor if you try anything. She has the evidence of your letters, and they are signed in your name whether you wrote them or not. Furthermore, everyone here heard you, and I don't think too many here would call themselves your friend. I suggest you don't try that scam again." She glared at him for a moment and using her peripheral vision she glanced around the room to ascertain if she could leave it without trouble. Her knife and her manner seemed to guarantee it. Sixty dollars though was a powerful enticement to any of these men. She had shock on her side and made her way outside without being stopped. She put the knife away once she was outside.

Cass didn't say a word to Stephanie as she climbed into the wagon and said, "Trot Stanley, trot Stella," and the horses after a few steps broke into a trot as Cass gathered up the reins. Neither horse was bothered as a horseless carriage went noisily by them going the opposite way on the street. As they turned a corner and began making their way north, Stephanie began to sob.

Cass handed her a handkerchief she fished from her pocket as she let her get it all out of her system. They passed over the train tracks as they headed out of Wausau. A second and a third set of tracks passed before Stephanie got herself under control.

"I don't know what I'm going to do," she said quietly as she looked around wondering what she *could* do. Everything they owned had been sold, and while it was a small sum of money, she certainly didn't have enough to live on with two small children and another on the way.

Cass reached into her shirt and pulled out the money she had gotten from Vince. "Vince wanted you to have this. It isn't much, but it's a start," she said by way of explanation. "As to what you're going to do, I have a farm north of here near Merrill, and I need a housekeeper," she said not expecting a reply.

"I can't let you..." Stephanie began, but Cass stopped her.

"Look, I really do need a housekeeper. I live practically alone, and I work outside all the time. My mom passed away a few years ago, and the house is going to seed. You need a place to live, and I've got plenty of room for the four of you," she grinned as she glanced down at the belly Stephanie was unconsciously holding protectively.

Stephanie absorbed this information slowly. She was stunned to find that Vince Lancaster wasn't the man he appeared to be in his picture or wonderful letters. She had a good idea how Cass had probably gotten the money from him. She was so grateful for the offer of a place to live that she sighed in relief. She leaned over and wrapped her arms around the surprised woman and gave Cass a hug.

"Thank you. I'll accept," she said quietly as she released her. Cass gave her a lopsided grin and returned the hug gently before letting her go. They both glanced back at the boys who had settled down with their hands in the crate and leaning against the baggage Cass had placed behind them. They and the puppies were both dozing off after their hard day.

"They look tired," Cass observed.

Stephanie grinned; she too was exhausted after their four-day train ride, changing several times, and the frightening events since they had arrived. "They are good boys, but this has been a long trip."

"You want to settle down on the sacks?" Cass indicated the flour, sugar, and salt.

Stephanie looked at them longingly and nodded. "Do we have a long drive?" she asked.

"'Bout seventeen miles. We will be lucky to get home before dark," Cass answered. It was a long way, which was why she didn't drive it too often. However, she hadn't wanted the animals to stay one day on the train more than necessary, and the little side train that would have brought the crates to Merrill from Wausau would have taken an extra two days for the freight. Two days could sometimes mean life or death with animals and poultry; she hadn't wanted to take the chance. She had waited too long already to get them. The extra money she got on her trade goods, and the money she had saved on her purchases, made the whole trip worthwhile.

Stephanie packed the money in her reticule and carefully climbed around the seat to the wagon proper to settle herself onto the sacks. Closing her eyes, she was surprised when Cass threw a blanket over her. She smiled up at the strange woman who had been her lifesaver today and saw something funny on her face. It was there for only a moment, and then it was gone. She settled in under the blanket, feeling its warmth over the weight of her jacket. She wondered if the boys were warm enough, but they had their coats and were out in the sun.

Cass drove along not really seeing where they were going. She trusted her horses, and they had taken this trip a couple of times in their lifetime. The woods closed in on both sides of the rocky road interspersed here and there with meadows. Occasionally a track, a drive, or even another road intersected theirs. Cass could see where farmers were carving out farms just like her own from the wilderness. Her own farm had been in their family since the time of her grandparents. They had settled in the Merrill area in huge deep woods so that Grandpa could hunt and trap while he cut down trees and carved out a farm that existed to this day. Her own father had enlarged the farm and added a small mill to cut the trees for their own use. He had used water from the nearby creek to turn the wheel that turned the saw.

His only disappointment in the farm was that his own son didn't take pride in it. Cal had turned wild, and his only release was in the trapping and hunting he did practically all year long. Cass's father had left the farm to Cass solely, but she shared whenever Cal was around. Cal had understood their father's decision and accepted it. Even he had to admit it would be foolish to leave him something he didn't want and would never use. The death of their mother a few years ago had saddened them both, as it was the last link with a time where neither had any responsibilities. Cass had grown up working on the farm, as naturally as most boys, and her father, at least, had been proud of her accomplishments. Her mother and father had been pleased with her natural abilities around the farm where Cal showed no interest.

Cass had started raising poultry, and even now, in the back of her wagon were new kinds to add to her flocks. She now raised chickens, ducks, and geese, mostly for egg and meat production, but these new and different breeds would enhance her flocks. She wanted to raise turkeys, but everyone said it was too cold this far north in the big woods of Wisconsin. She wanted to prove them wrong but would wait until next year. She had enough on her plate with the plowing, seeding, weeding, cultivating, and harvesting. She did it all, and she did it alone. Now, she had Stephanie Evans and her children. She didn't know why fate had put them in her path, but she hadn't lied about needing a housekeeper. She didn't need the added mouths of Stephanie and her children, but she had an affinity for children and enjoyed them. Maybe God had put them in her path for a reason. She would wait and see. Deep down a momentary thought crossed her mind, but she quickly dismissed it and thought about other things.

The miles passed, and it gave her a lot of time to think. The horses were very strong and the wagon no effort for them to pull. They were also expertly trained by Cass, so she didn't worry that her hands weren't tight on the reins. She watched Stella a little more closely than Stanley, since she was due next month to foal. She had considered leaving her home but didn't want to drive Stanley single. Besides, she knew that Stella might hurt herself if left behind since she had been teamed with Stanley since they were both foals. Stanley, too, was a mare, but Cass had called her Stanley since the name seemed to fit. She didn't know why Stanley wasn't also with foal since she had bred both of them to a Belgian stud over at Dahlmer's in Brokaw. It had killed her to pay a whole fifty cents for each of them to be bred, only to find that Stanley hadn't taken. Well, she couldn't afford to have her own Belgian stud, so she had to pay to have her horses bred. She knew that Dahlmer's would let her breed Stanley again for free since the first time hadn't taken, but Stanley hadn't come into season again. She would have to wait.

The added poultry to her flocks wouldn't require much more work, but she wondered about putting in more feed for her stock, as well as for her new housemates. Kids didn't eat much, but then, they were always growing, so who knew? They wouldn't take up much room, and she had plenty. Grandpa had built the house himself, and it had three bedrooms upstairs: a large long one that had always been referred to as the boy's room, as it stretched out the length of the kitchen; a smaller one over the living room for the girls; and a third over the den that had been her parents' bedroom and before them her grandparents, a fair-sized room with a queen-sized bed and matching furniture. Grandpa had bought this set for her parents when they married. Cass had turned a fourth and smaller room into an indoor bathroom with modern plumbing. It even had running water! She enjoyed a good soak in the tub, and it was heaven after a hard day's work to sit and ponder. She liked it more in winter, when she no longer had to make the long trip to the privy out back. The pipes now led to empty into the large lime-lined pit that had once had a shack over it. She had a second and smaller "powder room," as her mother had called it, downstairs behind the kitchen by the basement door. It contained no tub but a toilet and a sink, and it was convenient for washing up. Her mother had welcomed both of these additions, as she had hated warming water on the stove for years. Cass had further modernized the house after her father's death by putting in a modern washing machine in the basement, so that Mom could hang their clean clothes on the line, or in bad weather, on the lines inside strung along the ceiling. No more heating the water and wringing it; the machine did all that for her. Hanging the clothes to dry was a joy after the machine took care of the hard work.

Cass stopped along a creek so the horses could drink long and hard for the remainder of their trip. She climbed along the wagon to fetch the canteen and fill it upstream from the horses. She made sure her poultry and pups had water and checked that the children were still sleeping. The trip had obviously exhausted all of them, and they probably had not gotten much sleep on the train. She made sure a tarp covered the crates. The sun, although it was early spring, was still hot and the trip strenuous for her new stock. The puppies were flat out and sleeping soundly inside their crate, just like the boys sprawled out beside them. She smiled thinking about her plans for those pups. She started the horses up again, and they were on their way as she wondered if these pups would live to grow up. She had a problem with foxes, bears, an occasional coyote, and even wolves. Although Cal had trapped most of them out in their area, they still were occasional menaces as new ones moved in. She had lost her large male shepherd dog last year to a marauding bear, and it had taken her a year to save enough to buy these two from a breeder. She had chosen a male and a female from different litters although she still had her female shepherd. She hoped this male puppy would live to breed with both her females, and she could sell the pups herself. A real Noah's ark she had on her farm. The dogs would sound the alarm and perhaps help her with her stock. She had trained Shia and her dead mate, Shem, herself. The bear had caught him with a swipe that had opened his skull and bashed him against the stone of the barn, but the bear's own life had ended with her shotgun. It was too late for Shem, but she had used the bear pelt towards paying for these two puppies. The bear meat had been welcome, as well. Nothing was wasted on her remote farm.

The sun was beginning to set, and she was tired herself as they began to drive down the long drive that ended at her farm. She woke Stephanie, noting that both boys were already awake and looking about them with interest.

"We're here?" Stephanie asked sleepily as she stretched.

"Almost, it's up there," Cass indicated with her chin.

"Where are we?" the larger of the two boys asked. He sounded frightened, waking up with large trees towering over them.

"We're at Cass's farm," his mother told him reassuredly.

The boys stood up to see their new surroundings, holding onto the crate for balance. They were traveling along a very long line of trees. They lined a large fenced field that had been planted in corn the previous year. The cut off stalks were all over the field. A cow and a yearling calf grazed and watched as they passed. A lone horse was farther out in the field and neighed in welcome when it saw them. The cows began to walk along with them, realizing that it was almost time for milking and feeding. The drive ended in the farmyard, turning in towards the house, which had been hidden behind a large hedge of cherry bushes. Two large trees in the front yard provided the house with shade. They passed a small screen house as they came around it to the backyard in front of the barn. Cass pointed out that the trees were apple and pear.

"They say pear can't be grown this far north, but my Grandpa proved them wrong. He said with enough protection from the cold winter winds, they would do fine." A large white barn dominated the farmyard. Beyond it was a silo and beyond that, a well house. A garage was across the yard with doors on both sides. One could drive through these doors to the other side of the barn, so that she could unhitch the horses out of the weather, and the buggy or wagon could be left inside. Paddocks lined two sides of the barn. The third side was taken up by poultry pens divided into long swathes and covered in wire over the sides and top to keep out hawks, owls, falcons, and the occasional eagle. The cow and the yearling calf, as well as a chestnut mare, were already waiting at one of the paddocks that led out to the field they had been grazing in. Snow lined the edges of the fields near trees that shaded it from the sun. Each paddock was lined with trees around the edges, and Stephanie could see where large woods once stood in the fields. The woods came right up to the barnyard behind the garage. A large woodpile of full sized logs and trees lay next to the garage and another beyond the well house.

"Why don't you go in the house with your bags and make yourself at home," Cass told Stephanie who nodded. Cass hopped down and helped Stephanie over the edge of the wagon. "Easy there," Cass cautioned as the pregnant woman made her way down. They both went to the end of the wagon and helped the boys clamber over the edge. Cass handed Stephanie her bags and then took the gate down to put the crate of pups to the side. "Could you boys watch the pups while I put these others in the barn?" she asked them.

Both boys nodded solemnly. Timmy, because he realized what an important job he had just been given, and Tommy, because he imitated everything Timmy did. Stephanie smiled indulgently; Cass had a real way with the boys. She realized Cass had kept the boys out from under her feet while she got settled and looked into the house. It was a typical farmhouse and painted a nice white. It had been painted in the last year or so; the color was bright and fresh.

Stephanie carried the two travel bags in with her. A large screened in porch, which now had storm windows up on the outside, was where she entered the house. Long, low shelves lined it under the windows where a person could sit and take off their muddy boots or milk cans could be placed or stored in a cool place before bringing them into the house. The house door was thick and heavy, and she heaved to get it open. It opened into the kitchen, and what a kitchen! She knew immediately she would like this house, just based on this kitchen. The kitchen was decorated in warm rust colors, and there was a fireplace at one end of the large room. A family style table dominated near the door with seating for six. Its top gleamed with a shiny finish. There were windows lining the side wall next to the screened-in porch, letting in plenty of light and continuing on behind the table next to the fireplace and then again on the opposite side. A doorway led to a walk-in pantry abounding with supplies and lit by a couple of windows. A large stove stood against this wall, and it was electric! Next to it was an old-fashioned wood stove, as well, with its chimney leaning to the side and out towards the chimney of the fireplace. There was plenty of counter space to the right of the doorway and a large set of kitchen sinks. Stephanie had grown up around farmers and realized this kitchen was set up to feed large crews if necessary.

A hallway went behind the kitchen sinks and cabinets. A doorway led to a living room and immediately to the left, a set of stairs led to the upper floor. Beyond that was a dining room with leaded glass display cabinets, displaying trinkets that Stephanie looked forward to examining later. She sighed; this was a home, so much more than the one she had just sold and left. There had never been money for anything, trinkets or otherwise, and with two boys to raise, never extras. Her own mother and father had been just as poor.

Another door was across the living room, and she peeked through it to find a warm and sunny den with the front door and a porch. It was the front of the house, with an extra wide front foyer, but it was obvious it wasn't used. Most farmers used their back doors. She closed this door again and looked around the comfortable living room. Rocking and easy chairs and a couch lined the walls, and there was a large wood heater in one corner. Windows seemed to abound in this house, and the curtains had been handmade, possibly by Cass's mother. A table held a large radio! She was excited as she had heard one once but never been in a house where someone actually owned one.

Stephanie returned to the kitchen and noticed a small closet in the hallway that led back to a small powder room. She took off her coat and hung it up inside. Rich woods lined each and every doorway. They were so beautiful they made her ache. They needed dusting, and perhaps polishing, and she vowed to be a good housekeeper to this generous woman who had saved them…who had saved *her* today.

Another door across from the powder room led downstairs. She closed this after discovering its secrets. Rolling up her sleeves from her traveling dress, she decided to get started. A meal was in order, and she could certainly cook. She found what she needed in the pantry. She noticed there was no icebox and then realized there was one out on the porch, where the melt would not get all over. She found fresh meat, which looked like beef, and cut off a few thick slices for their dinner.

She cut up and fried potatoes and opened a canned jar of beans, as she pan-fried the beef. She wondered if Cass canned all this herself, as the shelves were well stocked for this time of the year. Even when most stocked up, the packed shelves surpassed them all.

TO BE CONTINUED...

~End sample chapter of THE JOURNEY HOME~
For more go to www.Shadoepublishing.com to purchase
the complete book or for many other delightful offerings

 ~ *Because a publisher should stand behind their authors~*

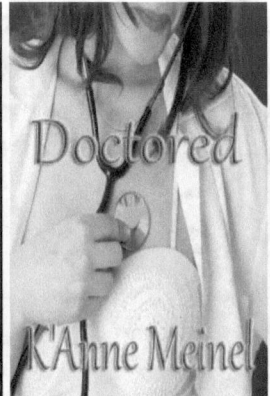

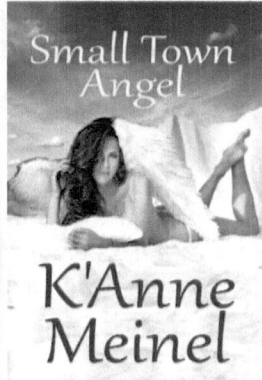

www.shadoepublishing.com

What do you do when you meet someone who changes everything you know about love and passion?

Paige Harlow is a good girl. She's always known where she was going in life: top grades, an ivy league school, a medical degree, regular church attendance, and a happy marriage to a man. Falling in love with her gorgeous roommate and best friend Alyssa Torres is no small crisis. Alyssa is chasing demons of her own, a medical condition that makes her an outcast and a family dysfunctional to the point of disintegration make her a questionable choice for any stable relationship. But Paige's heart is no longer her own. She must now battle the prejudices of her family, friends, and church and come to peace with her new sexuality before she can hope to win the affections of the woman of her dreams. But will love be enough?

www.shadoepublishing.com

~ Because a publisher should stand behind their authors~

When Delaney Delacroix is called to locate a missing girl, she never plans on getting caught up with a human trafficking investigation or with the local witch. Meeting with Raelin Montrose changes her life in so many ways that Delaney isn't sure that this isn't destiny.

Raelin Montrose is a practicing Wiccan, and when the ley lines that run under her home tell her that someone is coming, she can't imagine that she was going to solve a mystery and find the love of her life at the same time.

Carrie flees from the demons of her present, trying to protect the ones she loves.

Frankie hides from the demons of her past, and the memory of loved ones she failed to protect.

A modern day princess thrown to the wolves, Carrie's only hope is the rancher who had spent the better part of a decade in self imposed, near total, isolation. Frankie's history of losing those she tries to save haunts her, but this madman threatens her home, her livestock, her sanctuary. She knows she can't do it alone, has she still got enough support from her oldest friends?

*If you have enjoyed this book and the others listed here
Shadoe Publishing, LLC is always looking for first, second, or
third time authors. Please check out our website @
www.shadoepublishing.com
For information or to contact us @
shadoepublishing@gmail.com.*

*We may be able to help you bring your dreams of becoming a
published author to life.*

www.ingramcontent.com/pod-product-compliance
Lightning Source LLC
Chambersburg PA
CBHW050936120626
46552CB00001B/234